THE RETURN OF SINESTRA

BOOK I OF THE LILY BLACK SAGA

THE RETURN OF SINESTRA

ETHAN HOLIDAY

Charleston, SC
www.PalmettoPublishing.com

The Return of Sinestra

Copyright © 2022 by Ethan Holiday

All rights reserved

First Edition

Paperback ISBN: 979-8-8229-0442-2

eBook ISBN: 979-8-8229-0443-9

CONTENTS

CHAPTER I

LILY

Normally on people's twelfth birthdays, there are parties, friends come over, and cake and ice cream are served before the opening of copious amounts of presents. For Lillian "Lily" Hale, that isn't how she spends hers. She has no party, no friends, and no gifts per se, and Lily isn't happy. But it isn't for the reason that everyone would think. It's because she's just gotten her acceptance letter to the world-class Gerhardt School of Magic—one of the most elite wizarding schools in the world, renowned for the great and famous witches and wizards who came from there.

And she didn't want to go.

As a Pureblood witch, she should've been over-the-moon happy; this was the school that everyone—*everyone*—tried to get their children into. More powerful witches and wizards had graduated from Gerhardt than all the other magical schools in North and South America, Japan, Asia, and most of Europe combined. Most other Pureblood children pestered their parents to send them off as soon as they began to display accidental usage of magic so they could learn earlier, although that never happened. Rules had to be followed, no matter who you were or how much money you had. You couldn't attend Gerhardt until you had all of the basic classes and skills down—reading, writing, math, and so on. Lily was the exact opposite of all the other kids though…and she even had a direct link to the school!

Her aunt—and also her godmother—was Professor Isabella "Bella" Black, a Pureblood witch renowned for her innate and extensive knowledge of the dark arts and how to defend against them. Being a member of one of the oldest wizarding families in the world, the Most Faithful, Loyal, and Ancient House of Black (which had quite the famous and storied history, but that's for another time), Bella was one of two professors at Gerhardt who taught Protections Against the Dark Magical Arts. But it was the most obvious thing about her aunt that Lily loved the most.

Lily somehow was lucky enough to inherit the beauty that came from the most ancient of Pureblood families. The Blacks were no exception to the rule. In fact, they were considered the epitome of beauty, if the newspaper and other wizarding media were to be believed. Lily had gotten this beauty from her mother Callista, who was Bella's younger sister. Lily's beautifully black, voluminous ringlet curls fell down to her midback, and she had strikingly piercing blue eyes. "Small glowing lakes," Bella often called them whenever Lily stared at her.

Bella had the same mass of black ringlet curls that fall to her hips, but unlike Lily's, Bella's eyes were a deep chocolate brown to the point that they verged on black, something she had gotten from her father—and Lily's grandfather—Pollux Black. Combining that with their creamy white, flawless skin, it was a striking mix of the light and the dark. It matched Bella's clothes and professor persona too, as she liked to say with a smile.

It was irksome in some ways to Lily, since Bella only wore a loose, long-sleeve flowing black dress with a matching black corset (a common article of clothing for all the women of the Black family—and most Pureblood families in general—dating all the way back to Victorian times), a dark navy dress of the same type with lace sleeves and a navy-blue corset, a dress and corset of various shades of gray, or her most "colorful" outfit, a white long-sleeve button-down blouse with a deep green corset and a flowing fluffy black skirt. The most color that Lily had ever seen Bella wear was a pure crimson dress that she had worn one Christmas at the annual Christmas party. But Bella insisted on black, since it was her favorite color. It drove Lily nuts, since she loved wearing color in her wardrobe—even if it was just an accent piece.

"Mistress Lily, dinner is almost ready."

Lily looked at the young servant elf who was currently standing in her bedroom doorway. Like all servant elves employed by Black Manor and other prominent Pureblood families' houses, he was wearing a tailored suit with the family logo emblazoned over the left chest. His large ears were raised in alertness as he stared at her.

Servant elves were a unique race in the wizarding world since they were cousins to the Avalonian elves and the forest elves of Europe. They were also the shortest in height, ranging from two to three feet tall. Lily didn't know a lot about them, but she knew that they were the most docile of the different elf races. They preferred to serve wizards rather than be out on their own, and their sense of loyalty to their employer was absolute.

"Thank you, Tweety," Lily replied with a smile from her position lounging on her bed.

The tiny elf smiled back at her and left to head back to the kitchens with a small "pop." Lily just didn't have it in her to tell him that she'd lost her appetite the moment she'd received her letter. She'd been eating less for the last eight months as a result in trepidation for going to the school. Bella wouldn't like it that her mini-me wanted to skip dinner. And mini-me *was* an accurate description. Aside from their eye color differences, Lily looked almost exactly like Bella and less like her actual mother, whose photograph Lily had only seen once before—not because she hadn't wanted to see her mother but because it caused Bella a lot of pain seeing her dead sister. Lily just didn't want to hurt Bella, so she didn't pester her about it.

And that just led her back to why she wasn't happy.

Her earliest months alive had been filled with pain and loss on unimaginable levels, so Lily was glad that she didn't remember them, as she was only an infant. Her Pureblood parents had been ruthlessly murdered just shy of her first birthday by a dark witch named Sinestra. Bella hadn't told Lily much about her or why they were murdered, but Lily knew that Sinestra was pure evil. She did orphan her for seemingly no reason. Her parents weren't fighting against her or even involved in events outside of having a family. Bella had confirmed that much before she had abruptly changed the topic on her. Who would even do such a thing to an infant?

"Lily! Dinner's ready!" Bella called.

Lily sighed and remained sitting on her bed, hugging her knees. A few minutes later, Bella appeared in her doorway, poking her head into the room, looking annoyed. But that expression vanished in a heartbeat as she took in the downtrodden look on Lily's face. When it came to Lily, Bella was the most loving and compassionate person on the entire planet. It could be argued, Lily supposed, that she was like that outside of the classroom every day. But she did have a unique view of her aunt.

"I'm not hungry," Lily replied.

"What's wrong?" Bella asked, walking over to the bed. She sat down beside her and draped her arm over Lily's shoulders comfortingly. Lily only leaned against her aunt more.

"I miss them. They should be here for this."

Bella's face softened even more, if that was even possible. A slight squeeze of Bella's arm made Lily relax the rest of the way.

"I know. I miss them too."

"I don't want to go." Lily pouted.

Of course, Bella already knew this fact.

Lily had been quite vocal about not wanting to go to Gerhardt since the moment the owl with her letter arrived back in January. Bella had come back from teaching for the day to find Lily pouting on the couch, the opened letter in front of her, and arms crossed defiantly. It had been one of the worst nights in terms of an argument, and Bella had finally told her that they'd discuss it later. However, each time was just more and more upsetting, since Lily couldn't convince her aunt to let her not go.

Bella gave a deep sigh before she slipped off the bed and knelt in front of the little girl.

"You'll love Gerhardt once you're there, Lily. You get to spend a lot more time around me than you already do, you can see the other teachers regularly, *and* you get to make friends."

"I don't want to go," Lily insisted stubbornly.

"Lily…" Bella groaned. "Please, darling, try and look at this reasonably. I can't home-school you and work at the same time. Besides, you need to make some friends. Gerhardt isn't that bad a place to be. Some of my best memories were made there."

Lily remained silent.

"Trust me, you'll enjoy yourself once you get there and make some friends."

"I guess so…" Lily wasn't too sure about that.

Lily loved her aunt more than anything else in the entire world, maybe the entire universe, and trusted her explicitly. But this was testing her. Bella noticed this and leaned forward to plant a kiss on Lily's forehead.

"I know so. C'mon, let's get to our dinner before it's completely cold." Bella stood and reached a hand out, which Lily took. "Tomorrow will be a busy and long day. We'll go shopping in Merlin Street for all of your school supplies. I have the updated list for you."

Super. School shopping trip. This whole entire trying ordeal just kept getting better and better. If there was one thing that Lily despised, it was shopping for her school supplies. Her introductory schooling—to learn basic things like reading and writing that she was able to do right in Black Manor because of private tutors—had made that startlingly clear. A whole day wasted getting ready for classes that Lily found boring. The only good thing that came from school supply shopping was the treat that Bella bought for her at the end of it as a present…or maybe as a bribe. Perhaps school shopping wasn't all that bad now that she thought about it…

Both of them were tired and yawning as they apparated to Merlin Street at the completely unrealistic hour of four in the morning. It turned out, as Lily had learned as she was complaining about having her sleep interrupted by Bella, who was equally upset, that when someone accessed their vault for the first time at Drawlincott Wizarding Bank—the premier wizarding bank in the Americas and second most secure bank in the world next to the Grinning Goblin Bank in London—a lot of paperwork must be completed. To ensure that they left the bank before noon and weren't stuck waiting in jam-packed long lines at every single shop they needed to visit with the rest of the masses, they arrived right when it first opened.

For the two women, that meant sacrificing their mutual love of sleeping in.

Lily still mostly had her eyes sealed shut as they walked—OK, Bella walked and Lily stumbled along—through the dark, tranquil street to the bank's outer facade. But the moment that they entered the bank lobby, Lily's eyes shot open wide in awe. She had always thought Black Manor was opulent, but…wow. The entire lobby was covered in gold, silver, diamonds of immense size, and marble…well…*everything*. The floors were a glistening white marble that nearly reflected your reflection like a mirror. White marble pillars dotted the lobby to the second story. The fronts and tabletops of the desks were also comprised of the same white marble.

Bella guided Lily through the pristine lobby to the reception desk that was at the far end of the lobby, passing the two dozen smaller desks that had young goblins counting piles of the various different coins the magical world had and marking numbers down on long sheets of parchment. They all looked as nice as a goblin could look. Content. The goblin sitting behind the elevated head desk, however, looked like he was disgruntled to be working. He was writing hard on his own sheet of parchment.

"We wish to make a withdrawal from our vaults, please." Bella semiordered.

The goblin didn't acknowledge them at all; he acted as though they weren't even there. Lily looked up at Bella to see her scowling at the goblin. It wasn't often that Bella was ignored, and Lily knew that this wasn't a good thing for the goblin to do if he valued his peace. Only after Bella cleared her throat loudly and demandingly did the goblin finally—and begrudgingly—look up at them. His eyes widened in shock.

"Madam Black, I didn't realize it was you."

"We will make a withdrawal from our vaults," Bella demanded harshly, all traces of her politeness gone.

The goblin now looked from Bella down to Lily.

"Of course." He smiled, revealing all of his rotting teeth to her. Lily had to resist the urge to gag at the sight. He then reached for a stack of rather impressively imposing documents on a smaller table behind him and handed them to Bella. She snatched them forcefully from his hand with a glare before leading Lily over to a row of small tables that was clearly for customers to use. An inkwell and chained quill were present along with a small velvet-covered stool. Frosted glass with the bank logo embossed upon it separated each table spot for privacy.

So, for the next hour and a half, Lily was signing her name on all of the documents that they had been handed, and her eyes swam from all of the ink on the parchment sheets. She'd lost track of all that they said after a mere twenty minutes. For all she knew, she had just signed away her firstborn child to the goblins. By the time she was finished with all of the documents, her hand was completely numb.

"Madam Black, this way," a young goblin said, leading them out of the lobby and down a hall to a luxurious rail-tram platform.

Two iron trams were sitting on the rails, one of them with a lit lantern and the other having its lantern lit by a goblin who was so old he could barely walk. Lily idly wondered if he'd drop dead right there… and what the others would do about it if he did.

"Vault number, please?"

"Vault 3717 first, then 3713," Bella said, helping Lily onto the tram and into her poor excuse of a seat—more like half of an upside-down coconut shell. Bella sat down in hers and gripped the handrails on either side of her seat tightly. Lily thought that seat belts wouldn't be too much to ask for.

"Hang on, please," the goblin said to Lily, making her grip them too. The goblin released the brake on the tram, and they rolled off through a tunnel to the vaults.

The most terrifying and exhilarating ride of Lily's young life followed as their tram car sped along the rails at a far-too-fast speed to be considered safe, and near vertical drops plunged them downward into the earth. The drops were so sudden as they came up on them that Lily could swear her heart leaped from her chest and her toes tingled as the sense of being flung into the air washed over them. She was sure that if you fell off of these trams, that would be all there was of you. Forget about surviving the fall, even with magic.

The vaults were extensive in number, twisting and turning through literal caverns that looked bottomless…and probably were. They kept descending in this oddly beautiful cavern vault system until finally, to Lily's great relief, their tram slowed to a stop at a platform leading to a smaller, much less grand lobby. Above the entrance was an old, heavily rusted cast-iron sign that read "Ancient House Vaults Section 4."

Bella climbed off of the tram and then helped Lily as the goblin led the way to a giant door with golden letters marked 3717. Both women wobbled as they walked behind him for a few steps before their legs could handle their weight again. The goblin placed his hand on the vault door as Bella stood back, arms crossed behind her passively. Lily watched the goblin as the lock on the door clicked several times. The goblin then looked at her with disinterest.

"Hand please."

Lily offered it to the goblin, who placed it on the door as well. The lock—no, locks—all clicked open then in rapid succession before the goblin removed her hand and began to open the foot-thick metal door. Lily looked at Bella confused. Bella merely smirked at her.

"You can now open your vault by yourself. Handy since during rushes there aren't enough goblins to remain with you all the time. Plus, several people don't like the idea of their vault being accessed only by the goblins. Trust issues."

"Oh." Lily smiled at that prospect. Looking inside her vault then, she gasped. "Whoa..."

The vault itself was giant and nearly filled to the brim with gold and silver coins, jewels, and several highly royal-looking jewelry pieces. She was *rich*! She stepped inside in a daze of wonder and looked around at everything that was there to offer. The piles of coins seemed endless as she stood there.

"Take your time. Will wait on the tram for your return, Madam Black," the goblin said before waddling off back to the tram in a hurry.

"Thank you!" Bella called out after the goblin.

"This is...all mine?" Lily gasped. How had she never been told about this? Then again, she had never asked. She should have known, given how Black Manor looked, that she'd have a substantial fortune.

"Yes. This vault—3717—used to be Callista's and one of the Black family vaults. There are twenty Black family vaults in this bank. The most for one single family. The Ryker family has nineteen vaults here. That's why vaults 2423 through 3777 are the Ancient House vaults. They have four sections where they are located, in this lobby here, and it actually goes far deeper than this," Bella explained. "All of this in here is your inheritance of the Hale fortune, which was moved in here when it was placed in your name and added to what she had. It wasn't much, admittedly. She had to give most of her shares up when she married. Long story."

Bella pulled a bag out from behind her back and handed it to Lily.

"Fill this up; then we'll head to my vault."

Lily did as she was instructed, filling her bag up with handfuls of coins. She mentally ran through what each one was in her mind as she put it in the bag. The giant gold coins were the highest value of 100 credits. Then there were the larger silver coins at 50 and the small gold coins at 25. The small silver were 10, and the small bronze coins were the lowest in value at single credits. Collectively they were just known as wizarding credits. She didn't know if each one had its own name. If they did, no one used those names, just referring to them as credits. Looking around, she thought it didn't look as though she had made so much as a dent in her fortune.

Only after Lily had the bag filled to the brim did she follow Bella out of her vault and shut the door, hearing it lock behind them before they walked together side by side to Bella's vault just a short ways away but down its own separate hallway.

It was deeper in the lobby with an older-style 3713 carved above the door with flaking gold paint coming off of the numbers. Bella placed her hand on the door. Lily heard it unlock the same way that her own had, but there were a *lot* more locks on this door than hers possessed. Pulling the door open, Lily's jaw dropped yet again. She had thought that her vault was big. Hers was *tiny* compared to Bella's vault. It had to be ten times bigger—at least—and filled with more coins, gold and silver cups, elaborate crowns with jewels inlaid, more jewelry pieces, portraits in golden frames, and jewels of all kinds than Lily had ever seen before in her life. Some were even too expensive looking to wear.

"Yes, I know, it's amazing." Bella smirked, filling her own bag now.

"Wow." Lily couldn't help but gasp. She was overwhelmed at the sheer wealth that the Black family had. To think that there were another twentyish vaults filled with this level of wealth…

"Come on. We can now shop, and they all should be open by now," Bella said, closing the door and taking Lily's hand to guide her back to the tram with the waiting goblin. Lily only wished that they didn't have to ride the tram in order to get out of the bank. On the bright side, at least she didn't suffer from motion sickness.

CHAPTER II
MERLIN STREET

Now in the daylight, Merlin Street was unlike anything Lily could believe or imagine in her wildest dreams. She'd been there many times before when she was younger when Bella had needed to pick up some much-needed supplies for the manor, but they hadn't arrived there when it was in its main busy period, always just before the stores closed and Bella was done with teaching for the day. What she saw then paled in comparison to the wonder she was seeing now. She was *amazed.* She couldn't stop looking around at all the different shops with lines of people entering and leaving them and had on more than one occasion tugged Bella to a stop so she could gawk at something new in the shop windows to her aunt's highly amused smirk.

There were buildings of nearly all types on the street from all eras from the 1600s to the early 2000s. Interspersed between each building was an assortment of trees and gardens, flowers, shrubs, and in one spot, a park with a moving fountain, the statues interacting with those passing by to Lily's great joy. It gave off the perfect wooded peaceful neighborhood vibe that Lily loved. Also being nestled in a section within the edge of the city limits made it feel separate from the nonmagical urban city a mere few hundred yards away from Merlin Street's edge.

To any nonmagical person that was passing by, Merlin Street simply appeared to be an abandoned gated community with permanently locked gates. It was far enough away from most nonmagical residences that they didn't have many problems, and what few problems did arise were easily repelled by the copious wards that created a barrier around the Street. Several nonmagical businesses were nearby though including a public parking lot which helped with the parents of Nonblood kids.

It was strange in a way for it to be nestled there, since the magical world was pretty much stuck in the Victorian era, and the nonmagical world was all modern. Yet, being in Victorian times worked perfectly for magic.

This wasn't the original Merlin Street, of course—that one was in London. There were various Merlin Streets spread out all across the globe, in nearly every major city or collection of wizarding communities that had a large wizarding presence, but all of them served the same purpose: a shopping area where the magical community could find everything and anything that they needed. From potion supplies to school and dress robes to the newest broomsticks for Verona—a highly popular wizarding sport—to wands and even an ice cream parlor with over a thousand flavors, this place had it all, which was extremely fortunate since Lily needed to buy most of what they sold for school.

After two hours of constant shopping and browsing seemingly endless aisles of merchandise, Lily looked over her school list. She had all of her required school books and potion supplies for beginners and had been fitted for her school robes to be tailor made (Markus Wilbur—

the master tailor—was able to use her old measurements, which saved time). She had quills and inkwells and several reams of parchment and had even browsed the pet shop and the pets inside, which could be purchased for Second-Year Transfiguration class as she waited for Bella to finish up her own supply trip.

The last thing that Lily needed now was perhaps the most important thing that she'd ever buy: her wand. It was the tool that concentrated a person's magic, making it easier to use. The most advanced wizards and witches could perform wandless magic, but it was very taxing—at least, that was what Bella had told her. So, her aunt and she made a beeline over to one of the older buildings on the street that was near the center. A couple of giant old trees were in front, giving it a plantation-like feel, and an old swing hung on the porch, which needed some minor repairs. The sign over the door read, "Mirando's Wand Shoppe est. 1807."

"He's the best in the business," Bella assured her.

Given the long history of his shop, Lily guessed the same thing. If you weren't of note on Merlin Street, you went out of business very quickly. Stepping through the door, Lily gasped yet again. It seemed that today was just one of those days.

The first thing that she registered was the overwhelmingly satisfying scent of various different woods that seemed to cling to every surface in the building. The second thing that Lily noticed was the sheer volume of small long, narrow boxes. They filled every surface of the shop. Shelves of these wand boxes, with tags giving the date it was produced, Lily presumed, went from the floor to the high vaulted ceiling (easily three stories high) on more shelves than Lily could count. There was a walk-around second-level balcony around the shop and a rolling ladder to reach those on the third-level shelves. There was a back room.

Lily couldn't see what was in it; however, she could guess that it was the workshop where the wands were actually made. For all she knew, there might be even more back rooms that were hidden by all of these shelves.

Directly in front of them was an ornate wooden desk similar to the one that Bella had at the manor in her home office, originally her grandfather's. To the left of the door was a little waiting area consisting of two leather couches with a small coffee table in between them. They looked comfy enough to sit on, and during rushes, they were likely very needed.

"Ah!" Lily jumped at the voice. She saw an old man with long white hair and a clean-shaven face, if only for a day's growth of stubble, who was smiling down at them from the second-story balcony. His robes were of an older style, so he clearly wasn't concerned with staying up to date with fashion. A lot of sashes and tying were involved with his attire. With how wizards and witches had drastically longer life spans compared to nonmagical people, Lily wasn't about to hazard a guess on his age.

"I thought I heard the door open."

"Hello, Lucius," Bella greeted with a smile. "My niece needs her first wand."

"Of course! Let me grab a sampling that I think will work, and I'll be down in a moment. Please, make yourselves comfortable and chat."

Both witches went over to the couches and sat down upon one of them. They waited patiently as Lucius Mirando grabbed several wand boxes seemingly at random from the shelves. Bella pulled her wand out and twirled it in her fingers, showing it off lazily. Lily naturally had seen her aunt's wand countless times before, but she found herself staring at it in wonder now, soaking it in. It was a beautifully crafted wand, no doubts about that. It was fifteen inches long, polished, and had spiral gold and silver inlays at the grip. A golden band was at the front of the grip with a diamond in the center at what Lily presumed was the top side. At the end of the grip was a bronze tip that flared out into a cone.

"Mine's hickory with a core of dragon heartstring," Bella explained, catching Lily staring.

"One of the toughest and strongest wand woods there are. Fits her personality perfectly. It is extremely loyal but prefers challenges. The stronger the owner's talent, the stronger the wood gets in its magic, making the wand even more powerful," Lucius said, descending the stairs. Carrying a dozen boxes, he headed over to his desk.

"So is hickory the best wand wood to have?" Lily asked.

"It varies greatly." Lucius chuckled. "Each wood has its own characteristics and will, in conjunction with the wand core, choose its owner. Of all the woods, however, the hardest to tame would have to be mahogany and redwood without a doubt. They have high standards of loyalty, and if it feels you are not the superior in any situation, then your wand will choose the superior, changing its allegiances. Anyone who is lucky enough to have one of those wands choose them, regardless of the core, is truly someone of great interest. If they can maintain their reign on it throughout their life, then they are destined for great things."

After having laid all of the wands out, he beckoned Lily to come closer and handed her the first wand that she would try for the day.

"We'll begin with this one. Thirteen inches, elm, core of unicorn hair."

Lily stared at the wand in her hand. It looked rather…plain. Ordinary. Lily wasn't impressed with it.

"Lily, give it a flick." Bella giggled.

Lily blushed and did as she was told. She flicked the wand. Immediately, a whole shelf of wand boxes exploded outward violently and onto the floor, destroying the boxes and creating quite the mess.

"Not that one," Lucius mused, staring at the mess disinterestedly. Lily set the wand back down on the desk feeling guilty.

"Sorry," she murmured.

"Oh, don't worry. Happens with everyone." Lucius chuckled. "You should have seen your aunt here with her wand search. Set your mother's dress on fire."

"She was understandably startled, but she hated that dress," Bella said defensively, a pink tinge to her cheeks. "It never had an impact on her eagerness to learn magic at all."

"No, but it was quite the scene. I think the only time that I had ever seen Eos Black that flustered in her life." Lucius laughed and returned to the wands in front of him. "How about this one? Twelve inches, vine, core of bone."

Lily took it and flicked this new one. This time, a jar on top of the desk shattered, sending glass flying everywhere, and the water inside spilled over the top of the desk. All three jumped at the jar's destruction and how quickly it had happened. As carefully as Lily possibly could, she set the wand down on the desk.

Lucius smoothed out his robes with the palms of his hands. "*Definitely* not," he stressed and then chose another. "Fourteen inches, holly, core of dragon heartstring."

Another case of wands redecorated the floor of the shop, several wands flying out of their boxes and impaling the back of the one couch. Lily and Bella dived for cover as it happened. Lucius held his ground, looking at the scene.

"Hmm…Fourteen inches, red oak, core of Pegasus hair."

And so the rest went, all of them being failures. Lily was getting discouraged, afraid that no wand would pick her. Plus there was hardly any of the shop left to destroy now. Bella was rubbing her back soothingly as Lucius returned from the back room with yet another wand box. This box, however, was different than all the others had been. It looked older, and there was a ribbon of gold and silver tying it closed. Lily was immediately captivated, feeling drawn to this one like a moth to a flame.

"I don't normally test this wand to anyone, but I'd like to today. Fifteen inches, mahogany, core of Threshra hair."

It was hands down the most beautiful wand that Lily had ever seen. Where she gripped it, the wood was slightly rough, but it conformed to her right hand perfectly. Just where the grip ended at the top, there was a ring of gold with a design etched into it, the rest of the wand being smooth and polished. Where the butt of her palm rested, there was a flare outward. The wood narrowed just before it in a beautifully carved wave design. All at once, Lily knew in her heart that this was her wand.

"I think we have a winner if the glow is any indication," Bella mused with her smirk in place. It was only then that Lily realized there was a faint golden glow around her and her wand. It was fading fast. Within a couple of seconds of her noticing, it had completely vanished.

"That's right. Be mindful of that wand's power, Lily. Threshra and siren hair are the most powerful wand cores to exist," Lucius advised, handing the empty case to Bella.

"Yes, sir," Lily murmured, clutching her wand to her chest. Bella quickly paid for the wand since Lily had already spent over half of the money she had withdrawn that morning on her other supplies. That done, they left the shop and began a slow walk back to their apparition point.

Lily couldn't stop glancing at her wand as they walked, marveling at its innate beauty. Lily realized that the etching on the golden band of her wand was a constellation, but for the life of her, she couldn't figure out which one. She made a mental note to look for it in Black Manor's gigantic library. Lily was pulled from her musings as her aunt suddenly spoke up.

"That's from his personal collection, Lily. The ones that were deemed too powerful and too independent to be sellable. Not many can even hold them without the entire shop getting destroyed. It shows you're really special."

"So I keep getting told." Lily smiled. "Can we get ice cream before we leave?"

Bella cackled. "OK, we'll get ice cream."

"Yesss!" Lily hissed, making her aunt laugh more while they changed course for the ice cream parlor that was gaining more and more customers as the lunch hour progressed. Lily could definitely get used to this type of school supply shopping.

☾ ☆ ☽

Lily was halfway through her ice cream sundae when she became aware of the copious number of other kids staring at her and Bella. They weren't bad stares or anything; they just felt…uncomfortable to be under. For her part, Bella acted as though she didn't see them as she licked her chocolate ice cream cone. If she was trying to make it so Lily didn't register the stares, it didn't work. Pursing her lips, Lily looked at her aunt, who looked back at her with a raised eyebrow.

"Why is everyone staring at us?"

Bella shrugged in response. "They're probably shocked that I eat ice cream."

Lily laughed but suspected it had more to do with her looking so much like Bella before it was about her aunt eating ice cream.

"C'mon, let's finish these fast. Merlin Street will only get more crowded as everyone rushes to get their school supplies, and I'm already craving some elbow room."

Lily did just that and watched the number of people arriving on the street double, maybe even triple, in the time that it took them to eat their remaining ice cream. It seemed that everyone in the wizarding world was converging on this one location. It was impossible logically, but the sheer volume of people who were appearing had Lily thinking that. It seemed that everyone wanted to get their things right now while the shops had large quantities and have ample time to prepare. Lily was certain that there would be another wave of students, the procrastinators, flooding the place right before school started. So when they disapparated away from the chaos that was Merlin Street at one in the afternoon, Lily was able to breathe a sigh of relief at having room around her to stretch out at last.

LOOKING AT HERSELF IN her mirror a couple of weeks later at the end of August, Lily had to admit that she made the school robes look good. The white dress blouse paired with her knee-length flowing black skirt hugged her curves, and her all-black cloak and hood hung over her loosely. The Gerhardt school seal was displayed proudly over the left chest on the cloak, showing the world that she was a student of the sought-after school. Her black-heeled boots were the only thing that she was wearing that wasn't purchased for her uniform. As long as their footwear was black and closed-toed, then Gerhardt was pretty lenient.

The uniform itself only got more lenient the older you got. First through third years had to wear what Lily was presently wearing. Fourth through seventh years wore a white blouse/button-down shirt with black trousers and their overcloak, and eighth years—otherwise known as the graduate program students—were only required to wear their overcloak over clothes of their choosing, provided that they weren't too revealing or inappropriate.

"You look absolutely beautiful," Bella said from the doorway. Lily blushed and ducked her head at that comment. She hadn't been told that often, although she knew that it was a true statement.

"Aunt Bella…"

"It's true!" she continued as she walked into the room and hugged Lily from behind. "I think you'd be even more so with a corset…but still beautiful."

"Corsets are inconvenient and uncomfortable!" Lily complained. She'd worn corsets that Bella had gifted her a few times for gatherings like Christmas parties where her aunt's friends—mostly fellow teachers from school—would attend, talk, and celebrate, and when she was little, coo all over her as "Bella's mini-me."

"At first. But once you break them in and figure out some tricks, it's very comfortable…and does wonders for your figure."

"Ahhh!" Lily complained and squirmed in her aunt's hold. "It's not allowed as part of the uniform!"

"I'd be more than happy to put in a motion to change that."

"Please don't!" Lily gasped, horrified.

Bella cackled at Lily's facial expression before kissing her temple. She straightened her body again, letting her go.

"All right, I'm done teasing. Let's go so you can get settled in your room."

With that, Lily grabbed her suitcase and Bella's hand, and they disapparated out of Black Manor on their way to Gerhardt together for the first time.

CHAPTER III
GERHARDT

Like most of the world's wizarding schools, Gerhardt was isolated away from the nonmagical populace. It was better that way for everyone involved since nonmagical people couldn't know about the existence of magic thanks to international secrecy laws that were heavily strengthened back in 1692. History had shown that it wasn't wise to have too many nonmagical people know that magic was real and just how powerful it was. As a result of this, 99 percent of all wizarding schools were located away in remote areas of countries with copious magical wards keeping nonmagical people away.

Gerhardt was the only exception to this since the parents who weren't magical were allowed to come and drop their kids off, but only if they had a specific password, and that changed from year to year. They also could only find the school for certain time periods four days the entire year. The schools were also all nearly surrounded by lush forests and lakes, as nature itself had proven to be one of the best defenses for them. Gerhardt was definitely no exception to this. The difference though was that Gerhardt was in a beautiful hidden cove in a remote part of the Upper Peninsula of Michigan near the Canadian border on the Great Lakes. There was nothing around the school for miles except nature, forests, and the works. For the top wizarding school, its location was a bit confusing, especially in the time that it was founded, but it worked exceptionally well at keeping it safe. In the end, that was what was important.

Hidden completely from view by additional wards that were considered kind of excessive, the massive campus was larger than most of the other wizarding schools. The elaborate grand mess was in the almost direct center of all the buildings of the complex with the classrooms and was where all of the students sat and ate every meal together at their individual grade/year tables. It was also the only place where the entire school would be able to gather together for announcements or major events—unless they wanted to stand outside. Three wings of classrooms branched off from the mess's entranceway in three different directions in a configuration roughly resembling a smushed triangle with shoots branching out of them similar to a tree's branches. At the end of one wing was a massive tower that reached skyward. A building that looked more like a mansion carved out of stone and had another tower that held the principal's office and executive offices along with administrative quarters stood a mere twenty feet away from the mess and classrooms.

Only one of the wings was seven stories high; the rest were only four or five stories, but the seven-story one was connected to the separate eight-story dorm building via an elevated stone bridge at the third-floor level. The architecture that was used on the bridge was simply breathtaking to behold. Underneath said bridge was a stream that could technically be considered a small river where wildlife—magical and otherwise—gathered to drink and bathe. At the far end, obscured slightly by a few trees, was a rocky hillside that stretched up three to four stories with a waterfall that was relaxingly trickling down.

Several other buildings littered the rest of the expansive campus, including a large greenhouse, a giant field—which took up a large majority of the campus and doubled as several different things, including a hangout in good weather—and a small cabin for their study of magical creatures (and that particular professor's living quarters, the only professor whose quarters weren't in the school who wasn't an administrator), a full-scale Verona pitch with extensive stands to fit the entire student population, and even a small village—named Fortune—a short hike away down the beach where only witches and wizards lived to help support the school and remain in their own little content bubble of isolation. It was completely idyllic.

But Lily's automatic favorite spot on the entire campus was the cove's pristine white sandy beach. It was picturesque and not something that you would expect to find in Michigan—perhaps in Hawaii or some other tropical location but not up there. Waves gently lapped against the beach, emitting a soothing, calming sound that drew you in. She wanted to head over and explore this beach immediately, but Bella's grip and gentle tug on her arm stopped her. It appeared that the beach would have to wait. They turned and headed into the grand mess, where Lily was blown away yet again.

The ceiling of the grand mess was an exact replica of the night sky, showing all of the constellations and stars that were in the northern hemisphere. Various banners of all colors representing the past graduating classes, at least fifty years' worth, hung down from the exposed rafters. Lily was sure that there were even more banners that were tucked away in storage, probably in the principal's mansion, dating back to when the school was first founded. On the banners were the total number of points they had earned in their last year and the total of their entire schooling at Gerhardt. The higher the number of points, the more awards and medals the class got. Every year, all of the grades competed against one another to earn the most points to win a trophy of historical importance to the school—the Gerhardt Cup—and supreme bragging rights until the end of the next school year when the new winner took it over.

Throughout the giant room were eight tables. An enormous, ornate U-shaped table stood at the head of the room on an elevated platform with a finely crafted podium in front of it. That was where all of the professors ate. One of the eight tables was only half the size of the other seven, clearly the table that was assigned to the graduate-program students. They weren't as numerous as the other years since very few of the graduated students felt like going another year in an advanced learning course just for an added chance at getting good jobs—a whole lot of work for an uncertain payoff, not to mention the added stress.

"Finally, it's about time you bring her here, Bella."

Lily and Bella turned at the voice and saw a man standing behind them smirking.

He was a head taller than Bella, wearing flowing obsidian robes that appeared royal with a high collar, yet at the same time were extremely practical for dueling. His outer cloak was almost like a trench coat, ending at the floor, and it flowed off of him in waves as he stood there motionless. Lily could easily feel his power radiating off of him similar to heat from a fire. She'd never felt magic that powerful before in her life. It was intoxicating and overwhelming at the same time. His dirty blond hair was long and fell in ringlet curls like hers and Bella's to his shoulders, and he wore a full mustache. His blue-bordering-on-gray eyes twinkled at them with amusement. Yet, despite his intimidating appearance, his smile was fond and friendly to them, the smile that you gave to friends.

"I tried to bring her earlier for a visit, Sirius, but she's as stubborn as me," Bella retorted playfully.

"Ah, fun times for you." He then looked down at Lily, who smiled excitedly at seeing him again. "Hello, Lily."

"Hello, Sirius—er…Professor."

Sirius Ryker was the other protections against the dark magical arts professor at Gerhardt teaching the more advanced material to the fifth years and up. He also happened to be Bella's best friend since they were infants. He was the one person who was like a father figure to Lily, even though she had only ever seen him at Christmastime or on her birthday for a few hours to give her some presents and chat with Bella. Then he would leave again.

"It's OK, Lily. It'll take some getting used to." Sirius chuckled.

"If you'll excuse us, Sirius, we do need to get Lily a prime room."

"Abusing your position in this school? Bella, I'm *shocked* you'd do such a thing!" Sirius exclaimed in mock outrage and offense.

Lily giggled as Bella rolled her eyes with a smirk. This was the playful banter that they engaged in almost constantly. Sometimes it would verge on flirty, but it was always fun to listen to.

"Come on, Lily. We'll leave Sirius to have his little tantrum."

"*Tantrum?*" Sirius scowled playfully. "I see no reason to stand here and be insulted."

Lily and Bella left Sirius there in the mess as they headed off to the dorms to claim a room before everyone else arrived. Lily gazed at the school in wonder as they walked and absentmindedly wondered what she was thinking for not wanting to come here. This place was amazing! She was pulled from her thoughts as they climbed down a set of stairs through the second-year common room and then finally into the first-year dorms.

The common room was decorated in shades of red, gold, and silver with royal-looking furniture littering the space. A fireplace had a roaring fire in it on the far side of the room, making Lily instantly fall in love. There were no windows in this room since they were on the ground floor and in the middle of the building of sorts. Behind the stairs, Lily guessed windows would be like on the other floors, showing off the stream and the wing they had just come from, but that was impossible for obvious reasons. There were two wings separating the men's and the women's dorms in a V formation, the women's on the left of the fireplace and the men's on the right side. A door was tucked behind some decorative drapes, which Lily presumed led outside. Emergency exit, she supposed. A large portrait of one of the founders hung over the fireplace. He tipped his coonskin cap to Lily in greeting.

There were several moving portraits back at Black Manor, often referred to as "silent watchers" in the wizarding community, but Lily was still in awe and waved at it. It was too bad they couldn't talk. Lily could only imagine the conversations that one could have with the portraits.

"This way," Bella prodded, leading them along the hallway for the women's dorms. "All of the floors have the exact same layout except the seventh, which has a smaller spiral staircase up to the penthouse addition for coed graduate rooms and a more intimate common room. You won't have to learn a new layout year after year, a bit of a plus in my opinion. You know where everything is and can just focus on your schoolwork rather than being lost on your own floor. Here's the best room that you can get."

Bella opened the last room on the left of the hallway and stepped aside, allowing Lily to step through first. The room was quite spacious with four nice beds and individual dressers to one side of each with a nightstand on the other that also doubled as a desk. A small stove sat in the center for heating and drying wet clothes in the winter—cooking too if they were in a pinch, Lily thought. But the thing about the room that drew Lily's eyes the most were three of the five walls. They were window walls that allowed a beautiful view of the beach and lake.

"Whoa…" Lily gasped in awe, soaking in every detail.

"The same reaction I had when I was your age." Bella smirked. "The goal is to make friends so you can claim this room every year. I'll be able to get you here plenty early, so that won't ever be a problem. But if you don't have enough people to claim it completely, then you'll end up sharing it with somebody random."

"Is sharing so bad?" Lily asked, making her aunt shake her head.

"Lily…you'll see what I mean soon enough."

She found that response a bit cryptic and odd but shrugged and claimed a bed. She began unpacking her things into her dresser. Once done, her empty suitcase stowed underneath her bed, she and her aunt walked back to the grand mess, seeing more and more students arriving with their parents.

"Go make friends," Bella urged one last time, almost pleadingly. Lily hugged her, and she headed off into the area where all the first years congregated, looking completely overwhelmed and in awe of what they were seeing.

Most of them had a mix of excitement and slight fear on their faces as Lily mingled. Some of them—like her—clearly hadn't been away from home for long or at all in their lives before then. Others were acting as though this was an exciting extended camping trip or vacation.

So far, she wasn't seeing anyone that she wanted to talk to or hang out with as friends though. It could take a long time to find someone like that, with many conversations. That would be a lonely few days at the very minimum. But there were people of all kinds gathered among the first years: pretty, plain, tall, short, thin, rounder, and of almost all races. Lily noticed Caucasian, African American, Asian, and then some mixes that she wasn't even about to guess at. Clearly some of the other Pureblood families had first-year students this year too based on the fancy robes like hers.

She was paying attention to a particular set of girls as they discussed different types of material when she turned and moved to the outer edge for some peace and quiet, having decided that she wasn't ready to be sociable, especially not to discuss cosmetics, material choices for clothes, or the like…until she spotted a redheaded girl looking alone and completely lost. Lily stopped and watched her discreetly for a moment from afar.

Given the Black family's notoriety for their beauty, Lily thought that she had seen the most gorgeous woman in the world in her Aunt Bella. This young girl, however, blew her and Bella clear out of the water. Her skin was flawless and appeared soft, her red locks were curly—but not ringlet curly like Lily's—and her attractiveness was unquestionable. She was so nearly angelic that Lily rubbed her eyes to ensure that she wasn't hallucinating. That was when the girl looked Lily in the eye, and Lily's heart nearly stopped. Her eyes were so green that they were practically glowing, and for the briefest of moments, Lily thought she could see waves in them even from afar, but they quickly vanished.

Walking over almost in a bit of a daze, Lily smiled politely, making the other girl eye her warily. It was crystal clear that she wasn't used to crowds and was tense. Maybe Lily could help relax her a bit…

"Hi, I'm Lily."

"Hello," the redhead replied timidly with a bit of an accent Lily couldn't place.

"What's your name?"

"Amara."

Lily now knew the truth. This girl was terrified. She smiled at her again, stretching out her hand.

"It's nice to meet you, Amara."

The redhead looked at her hand a moment before she gingerly shook it. Her hand was warm, and Lily was momentarily drawn into the other girl's delicious scent. "I'm looking for roommates, so are you interested in bunking with me?"

"Bunking?" Amara asked, confused.

"I mean sharing a room. I've already claimed one with a view of the cove here," Lily said, gesturing to the water behind the redhead.

Amara immediately perked up at that. "Yes, I'd like to share."

"Awesome! Now we just need to find two more people—"

"You must be Lillian Hale! It's hard to miss you! You look exactly like Professor Isabella Black. She is your aunt, right?"

Lily whipped around in shock, seeing another girl standing there smiling at her and Amara nervously. "I read about you in an old news article, the one about your parents' unfortunate deaths."

"Yes…you are?" Lily wasn't used to others knowing so much about her when they had never met. It made her uncomfortable. The other girl blushed and glanced away. She was slightly shorter than Lily with wavy-bordering-on-curly brown hair and beautiful hazel eyes. She also had braces on her teeth, giving her a nerdy appearance.

"Oh, um, I'm Sierra Rossi."

"Well, I wasn't aware I was discussed in any news article, but, yes, I am Lily Hale. This is Amara."

"Hello," Amara said, eyeing the girl with curiosity and slight wariness.

"Hi." It was then Lily realized the girl—Sierra—had a book in her arms that she was clutching to her chest protectively.

"What's the book?" Sierra turned it around to show the cover.

"Oh, *Gerhardt School throughout the Years: A Brief History.* I wanted to know all I could before I got here."

"Smart." Lily smiled kindly and fondly.

Sierra blushed shyly.

"I've always loved reading. I'm kinda known to my nonmagical friends as a bookworm."

"Well, we're looking for roommates. Wanna share with us?" Lily asked.

Sierra merely blinked at her. "You…want me to share with you?"

"Yeah." Lily shrugged. "We all need some friends, and since we're sharing rooms, this kills two birds with one stone. Metaphorically, not literally. Why would anyone just kill birds for the heck of it?"

"But I'm…um…" Sierra looked away and clinched her book tighter to her chest. "I'm a Nonblood."

Oh…Lily now saw Sierra's concern.

Although Lily hadn't seen it personally, she was aware of the blood-purity ideas that a great many Purebloods and Halfbloods shared toward Nonbloods—in essence, that they were inferior, a disgrace to magic, and rats for having claimed themselves magical and using magic. Those ideas weren't that widespread or popular anymore, at least in North America, but Lily knew that Sinestra was someone who shared those views…among a great many others. It was about the only thing about Sinestra that Bella had told her, albeit in a roundabout, accidental way.

Nonblood was also another term used to describe nonmagical people. It was often used like a slur, even though it technically wasn't. Lily shrugged at Sierra, knowing that she needed to calm the young girl down. She was getting more and more nervous, meaning that she had already run into a blood supremacist at some point. This would determine if Sierra would be friends with her she was sure, and Lily wanted her to be.

"And?"

"You…you really don't care?" Sierra asked, frowning in confusion.

"Why would I care about blood purity? It's bigoted, outdated, and stupid. I only judge based on a person's character and actions. That's what Aunt Bella taught me to do. It's the right thing to do. Besides, you find out a lot about a person that way. We're more than just a cover to a book, as they say."

Sierra and Amara both beamed at her statement before the three of them moved off together through the crowd of at least a couple hundred first years. By that time, most of the older students had vanished from sight—most likely to the dorms to fight for the prime rooms and to get settled. All of the first years remained huddled together as various professors kept them corralled like sheep in a group preventing them from wandering too far. Lily and her new friends halted for a moment, looking around when a passing conversation caught Lily's interest.

"No, that's not how it works."

Lily tilted her head slightly to listen in.

"Is too. My parents told me."

"Well, they're wrong. The Magical Congress has absolutely no say in which students Gerhardt accepts on their blood status. My mom works as a high Congress official. Besides, look at all the problems that train of thought has gotten our world into in the past."

"Whatever."

Lily finally looked to see one boy (clearly a privileged Pureblood) walking away in a huff and another glaring after him in annoyance. If looks could kill…

The one glaring was clearly athletic with dirty-blond hair and brown eyes. He was also slim but muscular and on the taller side. He had a small crescent-shaped scar over his left eyebrow, which drew Lily's gaze for a moment.

"Jerk," he muttered before noticing Lily looking at him. He tensed. He was expecting her to fight him on his views next, Lily supposed. She walked over to him with Sierra and Amara flanking her in tow, although more in interest at Lily's move than anything.

"Hi. What's your name?" Lily asked curiously.

"Scott Halifax. My friends call me Scotty." He eyed Sierra and then Amara now.

"Well, Scotty, you'll fit right in with us fantastically," Sierra remarked, making him blink at them in shock. His body relaxed from its tense pose as he saw all three of them smiling happily at him.

Hmm…Lily wasn't the only one who had listened in it seemed.

"We can't room together, however, so don't get any ideas," Lily teased with a smile, making him laugh, and his body relaxed the rest of the way. "I'm Lily. This is Sierra and Amara."

"Pleased to meet you all," Scotty said and smiled. "To be honest, you're the fastest and smoothest friends I think I've ever made in my life!"

"Likewise," Sierra said thoughtfully.

"First friends for me," Amara said quietly.

Lily wrapped an arm around Amara's shoulders, making her tense up at the sudden contact.

"Same for me. With Aunt Bella working here, I never really got to leave Black Manor that much, so I was pretty isolated growing up. Proof that money can't buy everything. That's why you all aren't going to be losing me so easily!" Lily teased.

Amara relaxed at that and smiled back in relief.

"Come on then. We should get to know each other a little," Scotty said happily.

Yes, these were definitely people Lily could call her friends. It was like they were all destined to meet and bond like this in a way. However, Lily couldn't help but feel that someone else was missing from this joyous mix. Perhaps they'd meet them yet today.

"There's some open space over there." Sierra pointed.

"Perfect! I need some serious elbow room," Scotty muttered as Lily became aware of just how crowded they really were in this spot. Were they in the direct center of this mob? Or had even more students arrived to join their fellow first years?

"I'll second that, Scotty. Hopefully they let us spread out a little soon. I'm beginning to develop claustrophobia," Lily joked, making them all laugh.

Even a few other students nearby laughed as they overheard her. So far, maybe her year wasn't as bad as she was initially thinking it was. They all just needed to break the ice with each other, as it were.

CHAPTER IV
FRIENDS

After the initial awe of the grand mess had worn off the other first years, the teaching staff of Gerhardt welcomed all of the students back for another exciting school year. The principal—Professor Sah Orion—gave a very long speech mainly to the first years, welcoming them to the 2011 school year and explaining how the school worked, the point system to earn the Gerhardt Cup (positive actions allow you to gain points, negative actions will deduct points), curfew, forbidden areas that no one was allowed to enter without a teacher, and so on. Since Lily knew all of this from Bella's remarks over the years, she mostly tuned him out.

Most of the other older students looked beyond bored as they sat at their own tables hungrily waiting for the speech to be over and the feast to begin. Lily's stomach was rumbling too, making its wishes known to her as the speech just continued on and on with no end in sight.

The principal was an ancient looking wizard with short white hair, older robes similar to Lucius Mirando's, and a snowy-white well-groomed beard that barely touched his upper chest. His skin was white, with only a slight tan from spending time outside. He had a kind smile and eyes that showed a level of wisdom that was beyond his years. It wasn't until he'd stepped away from the podium though that Lily saw that he had to be five foot nothing tall—not the shortest person by any means but definitely shorter than the height considered normal by society. After the conclusion of his speech, the food magically shimmered into existence on all of the tables, snapping everyone out of their bored trances and daydreams as they looked over all of the selections, which consisted of everything and anything they could want. The scents alone had Lily salivating as she eyed everything in front of her on the table.

After giving herself a large helping of mashed potatoes, gravy, steak, and creamed corn, along with a dinner roll and her goblet of juice, she turned to her new friends and the very pleasant conversation they were having. Sierra and Scotty—whom Lily discovered was a Halfblood—were telling them about nonmagical things and what life was like in that world. Since Lily's experience and knowledge of nonmagical things was minimal to nonexistent, she listened attentively to them talk. It wasn't that she didn't know about it at all—Black Manor did have a Nonblood television and DVD player—she just wasn't as exposed to it as she would like. Amara was equally fascinated by this other world so different from the magical world. The redhead was asking copious amounts of questions, which Sierra and Scotty were more than happy to answer.

Lily once again marveled at how their little group fit together so seamlessly, like they'd already known one another their entire lives and were just meeting back up again. On more than one occasion, Lily had glanced to the front of the mess where all of the professors were sitting to see Bella watching her with a small smile. Sirius sat beside her, smiling at Lily too. She wasn't sure if she or Bella had been more nervous about her coming here. Of course, on one level, it was extremely comforting that her aunt was still with her at school. However, on another level, she was afraid of being used by other students to get into her aunt's good graces or to escape punishment for trouble that they'd gotten into. As if she didn't have enough stress on her already.

As the dinner concluded for everybody, the principal stepped back up to his podium, drawing the attention of everyone gathered yet again and quieting down the room without a gesture or action.

"Before we conclude the feast and depart for our rooms for the evening, some final announcements. First off, the strict antibullying policy that the school holds in high regard is still in effect, and any violator will be dealt with severely by the staff. This is an all-inclusive school, and everyone is welcome here regardless of blood status or what that individual happens to be. We have hosted several hybrids in the past—and creatures—and take pride in teaching everyone who is accepted into this school. Secondly, first years, there are several magical beasts on school grounds that are inherently dangerous. Be cautious around them all and never venture into the deeper parts of the woods alone. Have a professor accompany you, although you should have no reason whatsoever to venture into the woods at all in the first place this year.

"Thirdly, tryouts for Verona will begin in two weeks for the second-through seventh-year teams. No first-year team exists, and first years are ineligible to try out for the sport this year. There are enough adjustments that you must already make, and adding this would be unwise for your studies."

"Aw, man. I was really looking forward to playing that," Scotty moaned quietly in defeat.

"Lastly, classes will delay their start tomorrow until nine o'clock for final preparations for your teachers, so enjoy your last day to sleep in. Good night, all."

Several students clapped at that last remark while others groaned.

Following the horde of students who were now all headed to roughly the same spot out of the mess, Lily and Amara got into a thoughtful discussion related to the creatures in the woods and their shared disinterest in venturing that far. Upon finally reaching their room at last, Sierra and Amara unpacked their things into their dressers and around their bunks—Amara looking longingly at the water occasionally—before a timid knock came at their open door. Lily turned to see a smaller girl standing there with her suitcase behind her in the hall. She had shoulder-length straight red hair and darker brown eyes…and looked absolutely petrified.

"Hi." Sierra greeted her first, putting the last of her clothes in her dresser.

"Hello. Can I…um…share with you? Everywhere else is full."

"Sure, that bed's empty. Make yourself at home," Lily said with a smile, pointing at the closest bed to the door. "I'm Lily by the way. That's Sierra and Amara."

"I'm Victoria."

"Nice to meet you, Victoria." Lily shook her right hand, feeling like the missing person was finally present, and Victoria smiled happily at her in return. Looking down, Lily noticed the sleeve of Victoria's left arm rise as she grabbed the handle of her suitcase, revealing a nasty scar. It looked like a design of some sort. Wait…That wasn't an accidental scar. This poor girl might have been branded. Lily struggled to hide her shock and horror at that thought and focused instead on helping Victoria unpack her things before all four of them returned to the common room, which was now filled to the brim with everyone sitting around talking to one another on all the comfy furniture.

Lily and Sierra grabbed a seat on the couch Scotty had already claimed as Amara and Victoria sat down on the floor by their feet. Victoria and Scotty greeted one another, and then they all continued talking to one another like they had been before. It was shocking just how perfectly Victoria had fit into their friend group. It was like she had always been present there with them from the very start of the day. The conversation varied, mostly focusing on their schedules for the school year and what to expect from each class. Protections would be easy, Lily guessed. They had herbology, potions, broomstick-flying lessons, care of magical creatures and beasts, transfiguration, and charms. Lily even got up at one point and made rounds around the room, introducing herself to several people.

One of the first girls that she met was Jane Kraussara, a Pureblood witch from a very social Pureblood family that was always the gateway to the wealth and prestige within the Magical Congress. In terms of wealth, they weren't one of the wealthiest, but they weren't near the bottom of the barrel either. They were around middle range, but that was still substantially wealthy, enough to afford the finest robes that money could buy. Jane was angelic in appearance with stark blond hair that collected at her shoulder blades in waves. The tips were dyed an emerald-green color that was clearly working its way out slowly. She also was wearing a necklace with an otter pendant upon it. To many, Jane seemed snobbish and had an air of superiority, but Lily could see that she was just trying to impress people. She was a good person at heart. She just needed time to adjust and relax.

Some others that she introduced herself to were Nick Kravitz, another Pureblood who was talking with Connor Surge, a Halfblood who actually was related to the singing sensation Goldie Surge—she was his aunt. Adele Farrah, another Pureblood, was holding court over a group of girls and discussing her viewpoints on an article in a gossip magazine when Lily introduced herself. But Adele was also athletic in ways that Lily had no idea anyone could be. She was already boasting about her skill on a broomstick and was sad that she couldn't try out for a Verona team this year. She and Scotty could be very good friends.

The last ones Lily greeted before she rejoined her friends were the Skylar twins, Katie and Jenna. They were identical twins and Half-bloods. Inseparable and of one mind was the perfect way to describe them. They never went anywhere without the other and could even finish the other's sentences without trying. They also had the potential for being massive pranksters based on how they were joking around, which Lily decided to avoid for the time being. They both were tall and thin with bronze-colored hair and soft chocolate eyes.

Just as everyone was growing tired and beginning to peel off from the common room to go to sleep in their bedrooms, Lily noticed her aunt enter the room from the grand staircase. Her presence stopped everyone in their tracks immediately.

"Everyone, listen up. This won't take long, and then you all can get to your precious beds," Bella said commandingly. "I'm Professor Black, one of the teachers for protections against the dark magical arts. I happen to also be your head of year, Class of 2017. In plain terms, I've been given the honorable task of being in charge of all of you and your actions. I'm not going to tolerate any one of you breaking the rules, so this is your one warning."

All of the eyes in the room were glancing between her and Lily repeatedly, making Bella roll her eyes.

"Since this seems unavoidable, this is Lily, my niece. She won't be getting any special treatment from me when it comes to leniency in breaking the rules. Buddying up to her for that reason wouldn't be wise."

"Yeah, I can't even get away with stealing a cookie with her," Lily commented, crossing her arms over her chest as a few chuckled.

Bella smirked at her.

"Follow the rules, and we'll get along splendidly. Every year from now on, expect additions to this lovely speech. With that being said, good night all."

All of the other first years peeled off to their separate hallways and rooms or remained where they were, wanting to stay up a little longer, chatting quietly. Bella remained where she was on the stairs, observing everyone with interest, but her eyes kept drifting every so often back to Lily and lingered. It was clear that she wanted to talk, but with her friends around her, she doubted that Bella would just walk over and chat with her like she normally would. She'd want Lily to bond with her friends first. A gentle elbow to her side had her looking at Sierra, who was staring at her intently. Had she missed something that Sierra had said?

"You can go and talk with her, Lily. We'll stay here and talk more."

"Yeah, go on. She's your aunt after all," Scotty added with a smile.

"Are you guys sure?" Lily asked nervously. She didn't want to do the wrong thing with them so soon. She had no idea how to manage a brand-new friendship. Not having had any friends outside of the school, Lily was in uncharted waters, and she didn't want to screw it up in any way.

"Go ahead. You want to. I can see it," Victoria said with a small smile. Lily did want to. She smiled at all of her friends, vowing to them that she'd be back in a minute, and then rushed over to Bella, who smirked in amusement at her.

"Friends?" she asked hopefully.

Lily nodded to her excitedly.

"Good, I'm glad."

"Aunt Bella?"

"Mhmm?"

"Um, we can still hug here and stuff…right?" Bella's eyes softened at Lily's unsure tone of voice. They hadn't discussed that stuff before coming here, and Lily didn't know what would be permitted.

"Yes, as long as it isn't during the middle of class or in the middle of a public gathering. Nothing's changed with us, Lily. I promise."

That was a giant relief. Given her speech, Lily was seriously beginning to question. Bella then turned her gaze to her new friends, who were watching the scene with interest as they spoke. They were probably wondering if they were going to hug or something similar if Lily had to guess. Too bad they were going to be disappointed that night. Maybe someday in the future they would be privy to that scene, but not that night.

"So who are they?" Bella asked inquisitively.

Lily gave her a quick rundown on each of her friends. It occurred as she was doing so that she didn't know that much about Amara but an awful lot about everyone else. She even knew more about Victoria—as timid as she was—than she did the other redhead. She had to ask Amara more questions later that night when they all went to bed and were still awake for a little bit. She didn't want to return immediately and begin to interrogate her. That wouldn't be fair to Amara.

❲ ☆ ❳

"IT'S A SHAME THAT classes are delayed tomorrow. It's better to just wake up and jump right into new material bright and early," Sierra said as she crawled under the covers on her bed.

The other three girls giggled at that.

"What?"

"You really are a bookworm, Sierra. And I mean that with love," Lily replied, still giggling. Sierra playfully stuck her tongue out at her.

"I think there's nothing wrong with a quest for new knowledge," Amara said, fixing the covers over her legs as she leaned her back against the headboard. Her gaze wasn't on anyone; instead, it was locked on the waves gently lapping against the beach.

"*Thank* you, Amara," Sierra said, nodding victoriously.

"That reminds me," Lily said, turning her whole body to face Amara. "I never asked you where you're from or what you are. Not that it matters that much what blood status you are, but we told each other ours, and you never had the chance to. Most of the conversation we had today was about the rest of us."

"Oh, wow, Lily's right. Sorry, Amara, we should've let you talk about yourself more," Sierra apologized, looking guilty.

"It's OK," Amara replied, smiling at the bookworm. "I was enjoying getting to know all of you too much. I've never been a big talker all of my life."

"Well, if you have a thought when we're talking, let us know." Lily smirked. "We can shut up for you."

"Very well!" Amara laughed. "However, that does nothing for the nervousness."

"We won't discriminate," Lily assured her.

Victoria and Sierra nodded their agreement to Lily's statement from their own beds. Amara bit her plump lower lip nervously.

"Well…I'm really afraid that you all will look at me differently if I do."

"I promise, Amara, I won't," Lily vowed seriously. "You're my friend, and nothing will ever change that. Even if you murdered a whole village or something."

"Nor will I look at you differently," Sierra added with a smile.

"As long as you aren't secretly an ogre, I don't care. Those things scare the crap out of me." Victoria shivered.

Amara smiled but shifted uncomfortably in her bed.

"What about if I was a siren?" Amara asked at last. She was so tense she looked like a statue sitting there on her bed. It was almost an unnatural stillness.

Silence filled the room for several heartbeats as everyone processed what Amara had just said. There was no way that they'd heard her correctly. But then again, it explained a lot of things about her: her stunning beauty that was too perfect, her glowing eyes with waves in them, the way she looked at the water…

Victoria was the first of them to recover from the shock, although the statement that slipped from her lips caused her to wince immediately afterward. "But you're not the evil, murdering siren you should be!"

"It's OK," Amara reassured her quickly, extending a hand to Victoria as she opened her mouth to apologize. "Most of my kind do act and are viewed that way. I'm trying to prove in a way that we're more than that."

"So that explains you staring at the water. That's all you've ever known until now," Sierra deduced. "You feel comfortable around it because it's your home."

"Hold on. I'm confused." Lily frowned. "I was always told that magical creatures couldn't become witches or wizards because their magic is different than ours. Unless they were half-breeds of course."

"That is true. However, some sirens have shown the potential. There are only three previously recorded sirens who have had the potential, and I'm now the fourth. My grandmother is a siren-witch actually. Her name's Scylla, and I don't know if you—"

"Scylla?" Sierra perked up. "As in Scylla Saint? The witch that created several new spells involved in healing cursed wounds and the mirror-image defensive spell? Also the witch who made the teeth-restoration potion? The only one of its kind?"

"Among her other deeds and accomplishments, yes, that is my grandmother," Amara said proudly and a little shyly.

"She even earned herself a coveted spot on a golden champion card! They don't hand those out to just anybody! Only someone with major world-changing accomplishments gets a spot on them, and even then, it has to be proven that they are talented to the extreme. A new card is made about every three to five years." Victoria beamed, making Amara duck her head slightly.

"I know I have big shoes to fill."

"I know you can do it, Amara. Besides, you have us now to help you! You can't possibly fail!" Lily declared with a giant smile on her face.

The tension bled out of Amara, and she relaxed back into her bed. For the first time that day, the siren looked completely relaxed to be around them.

"I appreciate the support. However, despite my wishes to keep talking, I think we need to get some sleep for tomorrow."

"I can't wait!" Sierra squealed excitedly in anticipation.

"Yep, bookworm," Lily said, earning her another stuck-out tongue from Sierra.

CHAPTER V
FIRST DAY

"Everyone come in and claim a seat. No pushing! This isn't a playground! This is a classroom! Settle down. Settle down!" Professor Drifus Bloodstone directed from the front of his charms classroom. He was a chubby man with a loud, booming voice. His well-styled hair and finely pressed robes offset his energetic and sometimes chaotic lessons. He was well liked by all of the students, not assigning anything that was too difficult, or deducting points needlessly for behavior like several other teachers in the school would—like for incorrectly answering a question when you were suddenly called upon, not having raised your hand at all. Lily was thankful that particular Professor retired four years previously. He treated them all like they were adults, but that didn't mean that if the entire class acted up that he wouldn't deduct points. However, Lily liked him for another reason: he gave out chocolate to his favorite students on the down-low.

She'd gotten chocolate from him at every Christmas party that the faculty of Gerhardt attended, and he always had a new joke that he wanted to share with her. Every year at these parties, he, Sirius, and Bella would get into massive philosophical debates on magic, and if Lily sided with him in the debate, then he discreetly threw another chocolate her way. It appeared that who he was in his downtime was exactly who he was in the classroom. A rarity among people nowadays.

"Hello and welcome, first years! I'm Professor Bloodstone, charms teacher. This class will be vital to your everyday lives as witches and wizards for the rest of your life and is a core class. I'll be teaching you this year the basic and most common charms that will be the foundation for all charms in the following years. So it's best that you all pay close attention in my class for your own benefit," Bloodstone began with a smile.

He flicked his wand over his shoulder, and several supplies—a giant feather and small stones to be exact—were distributed to each student desk. Lily examined both and was confused as to why they'd be given these for class that day. They hadn't even performed any deliberate magic yet.

"Today we'll be learning two very key spells: a levitation spell and a self-moving charm. The rock is for levitation, the feather as a stand-in quill. Seems logical enough, but in the past, some unfortunate students have done the opposite, leading to a pummeling of a fellow student via the rock or the charm not working at all on the stone. I hope you're all intelligent enough to have and use common sense such as this," Bloodstone said, eyeing several students. "Let's go over the spells and the wand movements first. Demonstrate with the feather first, if you please, no wands."

After several minutes of students working on the pronunciation and the movement they would do with their wand, Professor Bloodstone gave the signal to actually try the spells out with their wands. Lily decided to do the self-moving charm first, and after three tries of various levels of success, she had mastered it. Sierra—being the overachiever that she was—got it perfect on her first try. Amara was currently helping Scotty with his own attempt since he was struggling with the correct movement. He'd taken the news of Amara being a siren just as well as the rest of them had, which helped immensely in easing Amara's concerns. Setting her feather aside, Lily moved on to the stone that was in front of her.

"Students! Be mindful with the levitation charm to not let your stone fly freely! Keep it in your control!"

Lily turned her attention briefly to those around her. Half of them were moving on to the levitation charm like she was, and the other half were still struggling with the self-moving charm. The fatigue that came with using magic for the first time deliberately was obviously affecting some of them more than others. Returning her focus to her own stone and the task at hand, Lily pointed her wand at it.

"*Volantium!*" Lily called clearly. Her stone rose shakily in the air a few inches before it fell back to the tabletop below with a clatter. That was a bit disappointing.

"Try relaxing your wrist a little more, Lily. You're too stiff with it," Professor Bloodstone advised. She nodded and tried again, following his advice.

"*Volantium!*" This time, her stone rose easily two feet in the air and hovered there as she maintained her control over it. Sierra duplicated that result with her own stone, smiling at Lily proudly and excitedly.

"Excellent job!" Bloodstone cried happily. "Five points to the Class of 2017 each!" He crossed to the other side of the room quickly just as a feather dramatically burst into flames, the young boy responsible blushing a bright red in the face. As Bloodstone rushed to assist, Lily lowered her stone again. Some slight fatigue finally washed over her from her exertions.

"Ugh! I just can't get it!" Scotty moaned as his rock stared back at him unmoving. It was virtually taunting him by not reacting. It was funny in one way and sad in another. Amara tried herself, but her stone only managed a slight wiggle. Lily placed her hand atop Amara's, shaking her head as the siren started to get frustrated.

"Amara, it's your pronunciation. It's Vo-lan-ti-um," Lily said slowly.

Amara nodded her understanding and pointed her wand at the stone again.

"Vo-lan-ti-um," Amara repeated slowly. This time, it lifted up off the table easily.

Sierra by then had taken to assisting Victoria and Scotty with the task. Scotty's stone suddenly shot across the room like a missile, narrowly missing Jane's head. She yelped.

"Sorry!" Scotty called out with a grimace.

"It's your flick. You're too aggressive," Sierra finally diagnosed.

"Oh…"

"A gentle touch is needed, Mr. Halifax," Bloodstone said, walking over and returning his stone to him. "Not brute force."

Scotty nodded. He watched Sierra do her flick, and then he tried again. This time, with his gentler flick of the wand, it rose wobbly a foot in the air before falling back to the table yet again with an audible thump.

"I think I need a lot of practice with that one," he confessed, staring at it.

THE NEXT CLASS THAT Lily found utterly fascinating was care of magical creatures and beasts. All of the first years were gathered outside in the field beside the small, modest cabin as Professor Kieran Raines introduced himself and explained what all his class entailed. Professor Raines was perhaps the easiest professor to bond with for students since he demanded a total of three essays (one being the final exam), and the homework was completely fun and simple. He also took great care to assign assignments that the students had the most interest in. The close handling of the creatures was almost spiritual in nature too, which was a welcome change from being cramped up in a classroom all day long.

He was a tall man, muscular, with graying hair at his temples. His skin was tan from all the hours and days that he spent outside under the sun, and he had smile lines at the corners of his eyes. An accident with a beast in his youth had cost him his left hand, which had been replaced by a magical bionic one of sorts. He wore a mustache and simple goatee, also showing some graying—giving him a rougher, more roguish look than his personality really warranted. He also seemed to have a natural connection to any animal that he encountered.

"Now, enough of the boring talk. Today we'll be talking about Pegasi and Threshra," Professor Raines said smiling and getting giggles.

A girl with short black hair, one strikingly green eye, and one blue eye—Lily thought her name was Sofia Jones—raised her hand.

"Professor, um, what is a Threshra?"

"I'll show you. It's more fun this way." He turned, put two fingers into his mouth, and whistled loudly toward the forest. "Lighter! Blackjack!"

A few seconds passed before the all-white Pegasus trotted out from the trees followed by an all-black one. As they advanced, Lily noted that the black one was larger than the white one. It had larger, fluffier wings and…Was that smoke puffing out of its nose? A fire-breathing Pegasus? Lily had no idea that they even existed. The others murmured about it as well, as both animals halted about six to eight feet away from them.

"This is the Pegasus Lighter and the Threshra Blackjack. They're mates, believe it or not," Raines said with a happy smile. "Lighter is a female, and Blackjack is a male. The two species are closely related, and offspring can occur from both of them together. But there are no hybrids. They either become Pegasi, or Threshra. An interesting quirk. As you can clearly see, Threshra are bigger, black in color, and puff out smoke through their nostrils when anxious, excited, or playful. As a result of this, they've been perceived as bad omens, or harbingers of doom. The mount of Death himself."

"Are they harbingers of doom?" a boy with chubby cheeks and curly strawberry-blond hair—Nick Kravitz—asked.

"Oh no. Divination would have you believe otherwise, but Threshra aren't bad at all. They're naturally very placid. Their magic is, however, incredibly strong. I know of only two spells or curses that will even do anything to them, making them an incredible animal. They also tend to not trust humans a whole lot as well. This is as close as Blackjack will ever come to us." Raines grabbed an apple from the bag hanging around his right shoulder. "Here, Lighter."

The Pegasus hesitated and then walked forward a couple of steps, before coming right up to him and taking a bite of the apple from his hand. Lighter whinnied before taking another bite and swishing her tail. One by one, each student got to touch Lighter and give her a pet as she munched on apple after apple. Lily was one of the first. She had moved off to the side to watch by herself as all of the other students had their turn. She'd never really admired Pegasi as animals before, but they were really something to behold. She could barely believe their grace and elegance. She was so engrossed in admiring Lighter that when her arm was bumped from behind, she jumped and looked to see Blackjack right there nuzzling her arm again.

Tentatively, and with deliberate movements, Lily reached up and petted Blackjack's mane to his delighted whinny. She smiled as she continued petting him, until Blackjack suddenly opened his gigantic wings and backed away from her, smoke puffing from his nose. Turning to see what was wrong, she saw Professor Raines was three feet away, an awed look on his face. The rest of her year was also staring at the scene, holding their collective breath at what they had witnessed, wonder in their eyes.

"Blackjack doesn't even let me close enough to touch him, Lily. I'm impressed. You must be really special."

"So I'm told, Professor," Lily replied, looking back at Blackjack, who was staring at her. Then he looked to his mate, who was walking slowly back over to him. Together the two animals walked back into the forest, ending their impressive animal encounter for the day.

❨ ☆ ❩

AFTER LUNCH, THEY HAD transfigurations with Professor Mercy. Lily was thrilled to see the grandmotherly witch again after several years. She knew that Mercy had been feeling her age catching up to her and wanted to enjoy her final years how she wanted. So when Lily and her friends entered the transfigurations classroom and saw a white twenty-something-year-old woman with shoulder-length purple hair instead of the short, brown-skinned, white-haired, wrinkled woman who was well over three hundred years old, Lily was confused.

"Take your seats. Don't be shy. I won't bite," the purple-haired woman said pleasantly with a smile. Lily and Amara sat down side by side at their desk as the rest of their year slowly filtered in. A small nudge to Lily's side made her turn to look at the siren.

"You seem surprised," Amara noted.

"She isn't the professor I'm familiar with," Lily confessed.

"Well, she seems nice enough," Victoria pointed out behind them with Sierra as her deskmate. Scotty—being the odd man out literally and metaphorically—had procured the seat directly across the aisle from them so they'd be together as a group still. Lily took advantage of this brief moment of settling in to examine this new woman more closely.

She was thin, yet muscular, wearing a form-fitted white dress that turned to fluffy skirts at her midthigh. It showed off her beautiful, yet not nearly as accentuated as Bella's curves. Over top of the dress, she was wearing a faded denim jacket that was clearly well worn and loved by its owner. Her chocolate-colored eyes were kind and compassionate, yet there was an undertone of hard determination, making Lily feel like she was more of an older sister than a professor. By then, they were all settled in their seats, waiting for this woman to begin class.

"Hello, class, I'm Professor Nikki Nero. I'm the new transfigurations teacher here at Gerhardt."

Lily just couldn't find it in herself to remain quiet. She blamed the part of her that contained the Black family blood.

"Professor?"

Everyone looked at Lily inquisitively.

"Where's Professor Mercy?"

Professor Nero looked over at her with a fond smile and warmth in her eyes.

"Hello, Lily. Unfortunately, Professor Mercy was forced to retire a month before this school year started after an accident with her pet Vixa resulting in her admission to St. Rogers Hospital for Magical Illnesses. But none of you need to worry; I've been her teaching assistant for the last two and a half years, so I know all of this class's teaching materials. Your education is in good hands."

Ah…that answered that.

Vixas were notorious for causing bad wounds when they felt threatened, and it was because of that few people had them as pets. They also acted out more the older they got too, and if Lily remembered correctly, Professor Mercy's was pretty old.

However, there was something very familiar about Professor Nero. She couldn't quite place what it was about her that was familiar though. It wasn't until after the lesson was over and everyone was leaving the classroom that it had finally clicked with Lily. Professor Nero looked an awful lot like someone of the Black family—like…eerily similar. Was she a member somehow?

"FINALLY, THE LAST CLASS of the day. I'm exhausted." Scotty yawned as all of the first years stumbled slowly to the seventh floor and into the protections against the dark magical arts classroom. The day had been excessively tiring since up until that day, they'd never deliberately performed magic; it was always accidental. Therefore, it was a blessing that their last class was going to be an easy one. Lily knew that her aunt never had first years perform magic in her class on the very first day. She said it wasn't fair to the students—or to her.

"I think today was a complete success." Sierra beamed as she skipped toward the threshold of the room. Her bag was virtually overflowing with books.

"Bookworm," Scotty mumbled with a twitch of his lips.

"It was quite informative. A good prelude to the coming year, I believe," Amara added with a smile.

Lily giggled at Scotty's answering scowl.

"*Informative*? I've done nothing but make a complete and utter fool out of myself all day!"

"Precisely. We now know that we'll need to tutor you together to help you. Very useful and important information, I would say," Amara countered.

Scotty blinked at her. "You…guys mean that?"

"Of course! That's what real friends do," Lily said honestly and in a heartfelt way as they reached the doors.

Stepping through the threshold, Lily was amazed at the classroom. It was a gigantic space with arched ceilings easily two stories high. On the far side of the room was a raised platform upon which two elaborate wooden desks sat at opposing sides. There was a divider between the desks, but it could clearly be removed to have it open. As Lily looked closer, she realized that there were spiderwebs glistening around them in the light. It was the oddest thing to see, and she couldn't help but stare for a moment.

Suddenly, Lily noticed that they weren't spiderwebs at all; it was the molding of the stones of the walls. They'd been charmed to appear transparent. Behind the desk on the left was Sirius, organizing pieces of parchment in front of him. Standing at the front of the room just in front of the platform was Bella, looking every bit the professor she was.

"Take your seats. We don't have all day," Bella commanded. "I'll dispense with the pleasantries since we covered that last night. We have a lot to cover today, so let's get to it."

Lily pulled out her quill and parchment, preparing herself to take copious notes frantically. Although the likelihood of Bella repeating something or even a whole lesson for her if she asked sweetly was fairly high, Lily wasn't about to risk it unless absolutely necessary. Best to keep her valuable capital with Bella saved for when she really needed it.

"Dark arts," Bella began evenly. "It is the most dangerous subject to study, because these curses and spells are used to gain power and control along with inflicting fear by these devoted dark witches and wizards. Most are openly frowned upon, and some are outright outlawed. This class has the singular purpose of teaching you how to defend yourselves against these curses, against dark witches and wizards, and against dark creatures you might be so unfortunate to run across in your lives."

Throughout the next hour and a half, Lily scribbled down notes for her aunt's lesson to the point her hand cramped up. By the time that class had ended, Lily was massaging her hand to alleviate the throb that she was feeling, while everyone else packed up their belongings quickly before heading back to the common room to deposit them there before dinner. Amara stayed with her as Victoria, Scotty, and Sierra went ahead, marching away straight for the grand mess and their awaiting meal. As Lily placed the last of her books back in her bag again, she noticed her aunt eyeing Amara curiously.

"Ready, Lily?" Amara asked.

"Yep," Lily said, standing. "Actually, wait. Let me ask my aunt something real quick."

"Academically related or familial?" Bella asked, suddenly right in front of them.

Lily had forgotten how silently her aunt could move when she wanted to. Almost like a ghost.

"Familial," Lily replied. "Professor Nero…"

"Ah." Bella smiled at her. "I had a feeling this particular topic would come up. How about we go on a walk to discuss it, hmm?"

"I'll see you at dinner, Lily," Amara said before leaving.

Bella stared after the redheaded siren until Lily cleared her throat, a little annoyed. Bella's nearly black eyes flickered down to her before her arm was around Lily's shoulders comfortingly.

"She's a siren, isn't she?"

"Yes."

"I suspected when I first saw her. Only a siren would be able to surpass the beauty of a House of Black member."

"Professor Nero," Lily said to reel the conversation back on track and to take her aunt's attention off of Amara. For some reason, Lily felt more protective of her than she normally did at her aunt's sudden increase of attention on her. Maybe it was because sirens were viewed as evil, and Amara could be looked at differently. That was the entire reason that she had hesitated in telling Lily and the others when they had first met.

"Nikki is indeed related to us. A cousin," Bella said and smiled.

"How?"

"My mother, Eos Black, had a sister, Arpina Black, who married Augustus Nero, and they had three children: Remus, Proxima, and Mira. Remus joined Sinestra's forces as soon as he could when she was looking for followers and was killed in battle shortly before the end when… when your parents died." Bella cleared her throat uncomfortably and moved on. "Proxima fell in love and married a nonmagical man and had Nikki, still keeping the Nero last name since she is now the heir.

Mira stayed single and is currently in Britain assisting with relations between magical creatures and wizarding kind—mainly centaurs. I understand that she loves her job. She writes to Proxima weekly, and she updates me every once in a while."

"Does—"

"Oh, Nikki knows. She hasn't been over for Christmas before, always having an excuse to give me, but you have met Proxima before."

Lily scowled at that statement. She didn't remember ever meeting someone who looked like Professor Nero before. Sifting through her memories, Lily was coming up completely empty. Honestly, she'd always thought that Bella was her last living family since she had no other aunts or uncles and her grandparents had died when she was four years old. She was just about to voice this thought when a memory of one of her very first Christmases with Bella came back to her: a woman in an elegant green dress cooing over a sleepy three-year-old Lily in Bella's arms. She could have been Bella's identical twin sister by the striking similarities, but this other woman had wavy dark-brown hair, not Bella's ringlet black curls. That must have been Proxima.

"I remember something faintly."

"I'm not too surprised you don't remember. You were super young when she came and were mostly asleep…when you weren't trying to hide in my neck," Bella confessed with a smirk.

Lily blushed and glanced away at that. That was an embarrassing personal memory. At least no one heard that aside from Bella and her. Trying to gain some control of the conversation, Lily cleared her throat and said, "Great. Another professor I can't spend too much time around."

"I never said you couldn't spend time around me, Lily." Bella giggled. "Just nothing too public. I have a certain reputation to keep, you know."

"But, Aunt Bella, you're nothing but a big softy with me," Lily said and smiled, earning a hug in response from the older woman. That was her favorite reaction from her aunt.

"Be that as it may, I am your professor too."

"I know," Lily said, melting into the hug. Who knew when the next one would be with her classes? She needed to take advantage of each one when offered.

CHAPTER VI
SIREN'S SWORD

The first month at Gerhart passed by smoothly, and everyone by then had settled into their rhythms. Lily and her friends were nearly inseparable between classes, studying together and hanging out in their rare moments of free time. Victoria would come and go in the beginning days, having made friends with others, but she soon remained close to Lily and her group as she fit in so nicely and naturally. Amara would hardly speak in class, and Sierra would try to be the one to answer every single question that was posed to them as a whole. It was humorous to an extent just how badly Sierra wanted to get the question correctly answered. Of course, because of this, several students were making snide comments behind her back about her being a "know-it-all," which did nothing but raise Lily's blood pressure.

So, as they stood outside in the sunshine for a change in their history of magic class, Lily was glaring daggers at the group that was whispering and pointing at Sierra. She was highly tempted to take the Black family approach to the issue—hex first and ask questions later—but that would only get her in trouble—with Professor Presnell *and* with Aunt Bella. Not exactly ideal. Let alone the potential of her costing her year points with that move. She'd have to exercise her restraint in this matter, despite how badly she wanted to hex.

"Now class, attention!" Professor Presnell ordered, standing on top of a rock beside the river to be able to see everyone. He was a rather bland man, completely the opposite of his younger brother, who was the current director of the Magical Law Enforcement Division. But when it came to his lessons and history, he lit up like a Christmas tree display at the holidays.

"Class! Settle down. We're outside today because of an artifact that the school will be housing for the foreseeable future, and its historical impact is *profound*!"

Translation: expect a thousand-word essay on this lesson.

"Can anyone tell me what…this is?" Professor Presnell gestured to the river, and everyone peered into its crystal-clear waters.

Lying there unassumingly on the rocky bottom was the most gorgeous sword Lily had ever seen. It had a jewel-clad hilt and a blade engraved in a language Lily didn't know and wasn't about to guess. It looked royal to her, like a ceremonial sword. The hilt was a deep-green color, and the blade was a mix of aqua and silver. What it was, Lily had no idea. Sierra, naturally, did.

"It's the—"

"Siren Sword," Amara finished, cutting Sierra off.

Everyone looked at her with interest. No one had bothered to cut off Sierra before, so they were in uncharted territory.

"Go on," Presnell said encouragingly. He looked pleased that someone besides Sierra was answering a question in his class for once.

"It's the only known weapon crafted by sirens for surface folk, or crafted at all. Forging isn't something that sirens do. It's regarded as the most powerful weapon in the magical world because of its indestructibility, and it only takes in what makes it stronger. Sirens guard the sword from dangers unless it's needed; then it is given to the individual who needs it. But only sirens and Pureblood wizarding folk who are of pure heart and intent are permitted to lift it."

"Yes! Precisely, it—"

"It has a sort of twin," Amara continued to Presnell's surprise, "that is well known since sirens also guard it, but it was forged by an Avalonian elf."

"Are you referring to Excalibur?" Presnell asked, enthralled.

Amara nodded. "The siren in charge of Excalibur's protection is always given the moniker 'Lady of the Lake,' thus the obvious discrepancies between the Lady being seen as good and bad in all of the stories. But the Siren Sword has no true guardian. Any siren near it has to guard it unless a worthy witch or wizard is in possession of it."

"Correct! Ten points to the class of 2017!" Presnell cheered. Lily touched Amara's forearm, making her look at her, finally tearing her eyes off of the sword in the water.

"We could probably learn more about it from you than the professor," Lily whispered, eliciting a perfect toothy smile from Amara.

"Or from a book. Oof!" Scotty said before getting elbowed by Sierra.

"Shush!" she hissed in annoyance.

"Although the Siren Sword isn't nearly as famous as Excalibur, it still has quite the reputation and a story of its own. There are many instances throughout history where the sword has played very key roles in magical events, and it assisted in suppressing the Goblin Uprising of 1412 in France!"

Lily groaned internally at that. There were so many goblin uprisings throughout history, stretching way back to ancient times, and in so many countries that the entire class could be about just that and nothing else. It seemed that one happened every one hundred to one hundred and fifty years or so consistently, starting from 11 BC. (She might have skimmed through the book and skipped over a lot of them.) As Presnell strayed off into this particularly riveting (not) goblin uprising, Lily looked back at the sword in the water, admiring it.

There was so much history in that sword, and yet it was just lying there on the bottom of the river, seemingly unprotected. Lily wondered if this would be the only time that she would see this sword up close. Most likely.

"So in conclusion, I expect each of you to pick one instance in history of the Siren Sword being used and by next class have a foot of parchment describing it. Class dismissed!"

"Great, another essay," Scotty grumbled while their group slowly headed back inside the grand mess with the horde of the other first years.

Sierra glared at him. "You need to take these assignments seriously. Otherwise, our tutoring you is for nothing," she chastised.

"I know, and I am! But this is the fourth essay assigned today!"

"So far," Lily added with her smirk.

"Which will take no more than around three hours to complete with the needed research. Less for Sierra," Amara said with a smirk of her own.

Scotty groaned, making all of the girls laugh.

"Just end my misery now," he moaned, throwing his head back. "I'll miss the Verona game tonight for sure."

❨ ☆ ❩

LILY ROLLED HER SHOULDERS backward, trying to ease the building tension from her position hunched over her desk, writing out her five essays for the day. Bella had added the final essay to the first years' assignments to Scotty's complete dismay. However, they all weren't as bad as he was fearing, just incredibly time-consuming. It was getting late, and Lily thought she really should be getting to bed, but tomorrow was Saturday. All of the students had the weekends off from classes, so it was their time to just catch up on their sleep, get ahead on homework and assignments, or just enjoy not having to go to classes for two days and hang out with friends. Bearing that in mind, Lily bent back over to finish her last essay—the one on the Siren Sword.

It had taken her longer to decide on what event to use than she had thought, so she'd started writing it late in the evening. Sierra had finished hers shortly after dinner and Amara an hour after that. Victoria finally waved the white flag and called it a night with just her conclusion to go. But Lily wanted it over and done with, so she could fully enjoy the freedom of the weekend without the stress of the essay lingering over her.

Besides, she couldn't break her creative flow now.

"You should go to sleep," Amara whispered.

Lily turned to her, seeing the siren still sitting up in her bed as Sierra and Victoria were deep in dreamland.

"So should you."

"Don't need to," Amara replied matter-of-factly.

"What do you mean?" Lily asked, scribbling down her final sentences.

"Sirens don't need sleep. It's nice and refreshing for us to do, like a shower is, but we don't require it to function. Only an hour or two a day is the most that we can biologically sleep for."

"Really? That's why you're always the first one up in the mornings?" Lily asked, setting her quill down.

Amara nodded at her as she lounged back against her pillows.

"The same goes with food. We technically don't need to eat since our diet is practically nonexistent. We only eat to fit in or to indulge ourselves. Also, we can't get fat. I will forever remain this perfect figure."

"Indulge yourselves?"

"Gold, silver, jewels, precious things. To us, they're like your chocolate. That's actually 99 percent of our diet when we do eat. Select seafood takes up the other portion. Of course, my grandmother offered me a bigger selection of food to try given who she is and what I'm doing. So far my favorite thing is a cinnamon roll."

Lily giggled at that before standing, stretching her body out, and crossing over to Amara's bed to sit on the edge. Amara tensed for a moment before relaxing again against her pillows. Despite the copious amount of time that Amara had spent around her, whenever Lily got too close without warning, the young siren would tense up. Given her limited time around "surface dwellers," Lily presumed she was just having a hard time adjusting to how they acted.

"You and Aunt Bella would get along great. Don't tell anyone, but Aunt Bella's weakness is sweets. I've seen Professor Ryker use cinnamon rolls as leverage against her to win arguments before."

"They are tasty."

Lily had to cover her mouth as she laughed to be quiet and not wake the others. Amara smiled at her, waiting for Lily to calm down again.

"You're not wrong," Lily finally managed.

"But back to you, you need to get some sleep."

"Fine," Lily conceded.

After she blew out her writing candle, she went back over to her own comfy bed and crawled under her covers. The darkness of the room swallowed her up instantly without the small light, being even more complete that night because of the overcast skies blocking the moon from view. Lily lay there in silence for long moments, staring upward at the ceiling and thinking back on the Siren Sword. Sleep was refusing to come to her.

"Hey, Amara?"

"Mhmm?" she hummed, making Lily's insides nearly melt in happiness. Oh, siren…right. Everything about Amara was designed to draw people in to her. Seduction and such. Lily made a mental note to remember that fact better in the future. That was why she tensed when Lily suddenly approached her unexpectedly. How had she not realized this before? She was smarter than this!

"You know how the sword came to be…don't you?"

"I know the story, yes. But you can read it—"

"I've looked. It doesn't say anywhere how the sword came to be, only that it was made by sirens, and it was first sighted in Wales Britain back in AD 439."

"Oh…" Amara whispered quietly. "Perhaps no one was told the full story. I'd never considered that angle. Given the time that it was forged and the circumstances…"

"Tell me? Please?" Lily asked, looking at the redheaded siren or her silhouette, more accurately.

"I…all right," Amara conceded. "There was a small lake where a group of sirens had gathered as their home. There was tension all over the ocean, small disputes and even a civil war among the kingdoms of mermaids for better areas of control. They wanted to just exist in peace without being drawn into the growing conflict. They were some of the nicest sirens of that time, not murdering any nonmagical people. But they soon discovered that their hidden oasis was in one of the worst areas of Britain for them to be—a nonmagical area.

"When the nonmagical surface dwellers discovered their presence, they banded together in a mob and went off to kill them. Of course, that wouldn't have worked, but the nonmagical people didn't know that. Just before the sirens would've had to fight or flee, a young Pure-blood wizard risked his own life to save them and used his magic to frighten the nonmagical mob away. The sirens were wary of this sudden kindness that he had awarded to them, but he wished nothing in return. They were taken by this, his kindness and compassion, and began to have the idea that not all surface dwellers are evil and to be wary of.

"It was several months later that the wizard returned to their lake, wand broken beyond repair, injured, and on the verge of death. He had come to the only safe place for miles after his attack to rest…and die. The sirens, remembering his compassion toward them, couldn't find it in themselves to allow him to die after his attack. So, they took him in and nursed him back to health. Since his wand was broken, and leaving their small safe haven undefended was far too dangerous, they together forged the Siren Sword for him. They crafted it so only those with his qualities could wield the sword."

"Pureblood and pure of heart," Lily remembered.

"Yes. He accepted the gift and left. He helped get sirens recognition in magical governments, and on his deathbed at a very ancient age, he returned one final time to return the sword to them."

"They must've had a great respect for one another," Lily mused.

"Sirens always respect when things are done or traded fairly. Most common is a life for a life. He saved them from a very dangerous threat, allowing them to stay in their hidden oasis. They, in turn, saved his life. They thought very highly of him. Still do, in fact, from what Grandmother says."

"They're alive? Still?"

"We're immortal, Lily. Only under very exact circumstances can we perish. Sorry, but I won't tell you that secret. Not now."

"That's OK. I understand." Lily yawned. She wasn't sure she would even want to know how to kill a siren.

"*Sleep*," Amara commanded.

Despite Lily's wishes, her body obeyed Amara's command as though there was no way for it not to. Her last conscious thought was that she would need to talk with Amara about using her siren powers on her... even if it was for a good reason.

CHAPTER VII
HALLOWE'EN

"I should really have chosen a better costume than this," Sierra griped as she stood beside her bed in her pink princess costume.

Two weeks previously, during the breakfast announcements, they learned that Hallowe'en would be celebrated, mixing both the magical and nonmagical traditions as a new yearly start-up tradition for the school. Everyone was instantly excited about this, and it was all that most could talk about for the rest of that day. Why wouldn't they realistically? The day would be filled with special fun lessons and treats for them to indulge themselves with.

"I think you're fine," Amara said plainly, wearing a cat outfit, whiskers painted on her cheeks and a headband with cat ears perched in her red curls. Even a stuffed cat tail hung down from the small of her back.

"I feel ridiculous. I hate the color pink! In case you guys haven't noticed, I'm not a girly girl," Sierra insisted. "I really should have spent more time looking for a costume instead of picking the first one I came across."

"Isn't that the whole point of Hallowe'en? The ridiculousness part, I'm talking about," Victoria asked, dressed up as Terri Turncase—a celebrity witch widely known for her adventures and expeditions into lands far away and discovering old magical communities that had been abandoned over the many eons.

"No, the point is to dress up in fun costumes, go around house to house, and get candy."

"Isn't that dangerous?" Amara asked, cocking her head to the side questioningly.

"No, it's…it's…" Sierra struggled with a reply for a moment, before she just chose the far easier option of changing the subject altogether. "Lily, come on and hurry up so we can leave!" she yelled at their private bathroom door, which Lily was behind, giving her reflection one last look over.

"All right, all right, I'm coming! Don't get your panties in a knot, Sierra!"

"You've been in there longer than all three of us combined!" Victoria tacked on.

"Are you redecorating the bathroom or something? Get a move on!" Sierra hissed.

Lily scowled at that. "Well, you would be taking this long too!" She opened the door and walked out in a huff. "If you had to lace up a corset! I hate these things!"

Everyone just stood where they were and stared at Lily with slack jaws. Lily stood there in an exact replica of Bella's black dress and corset. She had to admit herself if it weren't for her eye color and slightly shorter stature (which another year or two of growing would eliminate), she looked like a clone of her aunt. Add to that Lily mimicking all of her aunt's mannerisms, and it really got scary.

"Wow!" Victoria gasped.

"OK, tell me that you're wearing that every year," Sierra said in awe.

"Not unless someone helps with the corset, I'm not," Lily said, crossing her arms over her developing bust and raising her chin haughtily.

"You could've used the self-moving charm to lace it up," Amara pointed out in a much huskier voice than normal, her eyes glowing brightly, waves visible in them.

Lily dropped her arms. She was seriously slipping in the intelligence department. She should have thought of that.

"Now you tell me."

Entering the common room, everyone did a double take at Lily as they walked over to the stairs. Scotty was already waiting for them to arrive in his pirate costume and stared at Lily with wide eyes. She permitted the staring for a few seconds to boost her ego a bit and then snapped her fingers in his face. As he shook his head to clear it, a faint blush slowly spread across his cheeks.

"Sorry. That's just…wow."

"Yes, yes, I know. I look amazing. C'mon, I wanna see Aunt Bella before we head down for breakfast," Lily said with a teasing smile on her face.

Lily led her group through the halls and up to the protections against dark magical arts classroom, drawing the eyes of everyone they passed—students and the few professors alike. Despite the corset, Lily was feeling the best that she had in a while. In fact, she was actually fine with the corset…just not lacing it up or down. But Amara's idea sounded good, and there was no reason why it wouldn't work. When Aunt Bella heard this, all Lily would get as Christmas presents was corsets. It was best that she keep this revelation to herself right now.

"I mean, you can't be serious!" Bella's voice called, making Lily and her friends stop at the door.

"Nope, I'm me!" Sirius's voice responded, making Lily smile.

"Shut up! That's not what I meant, and you know it," Bella snarled but without the bite.

"I think my costume is perfect."

"Oh, please, you don't even look like the real thing. You're embarrassing yourself! Go change before someone sees you!"

"Stop it! Besides, *you're* the one who isn't participating! Show your inner kid again! You always had the best costumes when we were students here! When we were allowed to dress up, you claimed the winning title every time!"

"Hardly the best," Bella dismissed, to Sirius's snort.

Lily winked at her friends over her shoulder and walked into the room.

Bella was in her usual black dress and corset ensemble, matching Lily exactly, while Sirius was in a lavish black robe with a crimson interior and had a set of toy plastic teeth in his mouth. He and Bella were locked in a heated glaring contest with one another, trying to sway the other from his or her argument point. It would have been easier for them to move an entire mountain. Normally, Lily wouldn't interfere in this and allow it to run its course. It wouldn't really get them anywhere if she tried anyhow…but she wanted to make an exception that day.

"Don't you have better things to do than stand around? This is a classroom, not a common room. I ought to deduct points from both of you," Lily said, imitating Bella, making both professors widen their eyes and whip their heads to her before gigantic smiles filled their faces.

"Oh, that's rich!" Sirius chuckled.

"And just who do you think you are, hmm?" Bella asked, playing along with her smile.

"Professor Black, of course. Are you blind? Can you not see the fabulous resemblance?"

"Oh, my mistake, Professor," Bella said, splaying her hand over her chest. "How foolish of me."

"I shall consider this an accident on account of the early hour. Consider yourself lucky," Lily said, unable to contain her smile now.

Bella chuckled and poked Lily where her corset was.

"Lily wearing a corset without me hounding her? I *must* be dreaming!" Bella joked with a wide smile and a dramatic arm flung over her forehead.

"Says the person who isn't dressed up at all. It's Hallowe'en, Aunt Bella!" Lily said excitedly, bouncing on the balls of her feet.

Sirius chuckled again, earning him a scowl from Bella.

"Lily—"

"Why not?"

"We wouldn't twin," Bella said and smirked.

"Hmpf!" Lily grunted, crossing her arms over her chest.

Bella inhaled slowly through her nose before she spoke again. "It is my choice to participate or not."

"But…" Lily bit her tongue at the glare Bella gave her. She had lost the argument. Continuing it right then would do nothing but make her position even more precarious. She slumped her shoulders and nodded to her aunt in defeat. There was no changing her aunt's mind when she'd made a decision.

"Stick in the mud," Sirius sniped at her.

Bella turned her glare from Lily to him now. Sirius, for his part, wasn't fazed in the slightest.

"I am not. But dressing up as a professor I feel is hardly appropriate to do."

"It's Hallowe'en!" Sirius retorted. "It's a holiday, so you need to lighten up. Besides, even Orion's dressing up! He's Merlin, or so I hear."

"That's not much of a change for him from how he normally looks. Just a longer beard and hair," Bella argued.

"The point still stands that he's dressing up."

Bella snorted at him. "I guarantee you that Callista would be dressed up right now."

Lily wasn't sure what to do now that their arguing had resumed yet again. But after Sirius's comment about her mother, Lily noticed Bella's entire body deflate a little. Then Bella looked at Lily and pulled her into a hug, which Lily greedily accepted. They hadn't been able to share many hugs since the school year had started, so she wasn't about to let this one escape her. She melted against Bella as her lips rested in Lily's ringlet curls.

"How about I dress up next year? Since this will be a new yearly tradition, I need to prepare my costume properly," Bella whispered, her voice apologetic.

"Deal," Lily replied, a softness in her tone for her aunt.

They stayed like that for another few minutes before Bella kissed her forehead and pulled back. Sirius was leaning against a nearby desk, arms crossed over his chest with a smirk in place. Lily smiled as Bella rolled her eyes at him. The playful bantering was about to commence yet again.

"You've grown soft with Lily." Sirius chuckled.

"Hardly." Bella sniffed, a haughty expression on her face and her chin raised. "We aren't in class."

"Technically."

"Truthfully," Bella corrected. "Besides, she's my niece. She's earned hugs and kisses by blood."

"And getting spoiled rotten?" Sirius asked.

Lily covered her giggles with a hand over her mouth. He winked at her, which only made Bella yell at him.

"Oi! I have not spoiled her! I'm not one of *those* aunts! I've been raising her since she was a year old."

"She's your daughter for all intents and purposes."

"Exactly, she *is* my daugh—" Bella stopped talking and stared wide-eyed at Sirius, mouth agape. She had just completely walked right into that trap without so much as a fight.

Sirius, however, burst out in howling laughter as Lily hugged her again tighter, bouncing excitedly. That was the best thing that she could have ever heard from Bella that day. Or ever.

"Oh, Bella, I thought I'd have to use truth serum slipped into your drink to get you to admit that!" Sirius laughed. "It's been *soooo* obvious for years!"

"I—that—I meant—I—" Bella stuttered in shock.

"It's OK, Aunt Bella. I'm happy that I'm your daughter in your eyes," Lily cooed. She was now in complete bliss. So far, the day was going great. Bella hugged her back, and it was at that moment that Lily's friends cheered from the doorway.

Bella jumped and then scowled, while Sirius bellowed in laughter again as Lily giggled along.

"If I hear one word of this conversation ever being discussed outside of this assembled group, I'll give everyone detention. Is that clear?" Bella demanded.

"Yes, Professor Black," Lily and her friends crooned in unison.

"Good. Now, we need to get all of you to breakfast."

(☆)

"I think Amara's a little taken by you in a corset, Lily. She hasn't taken her eyes off of you all day," Scotty teased as Victoria and Sierra snickered at them.

Lily blushed faintly as Amara pried her eyes off of her, suddenly finding the ceiling very interesting.

"I have the Black family beauty, so I'm, um, not too surprised. Besides, it does wonders for my figure," Lily replied. She tried to play it off as nothing, but she felt her blush only increasing.

"I think a crush has formed," Sierra added.

"We're only twelve," Lily retorted.

"So? Love knows no age," Scotty said boldly.

Lily glanced at Amara, making both of them blush a deep red, almost the color of the siren's hair. They weren't ready to have this conversation, and the teasing certainly wasn't helping. A change of subject was in order.

"Even though it's still some time away yet, what are you guys doing for Christmas?" Lily asked after she had cleared her throat.

"Going home to my mom. She has the entire break off." Scotty beamed. "Being a high member of the Magical Congress, her time off is really scarce. There's always something that needs to be done, you know. I'm really looking forward to it being me and her with no business."

"I'm going home to my parents as well," Sierra sang. It was clear that she was happy to see her parents again after all this time, even though they all were so close. There was something special about parents that no matter how close you were with your friends, you just couldn't replace it. Lily had to base her feelings about parents off of Bella, given her history, but she considered Bella an awesome mom.

"I'll be staying," Victoria sounded relieved by that fact as she said it. Lily didn't question her.

"I am staying as well. My mother isn't pleased with me coming to Gerhardt at all, so Grandmother said it would be wise if I didn't return until school was over for the summer. It would result in less drama," Amara said, fluffing her red curls. Her emerald eyes were still glowing with waves in them, but her blush had thankfully vanished.

"What about you, Lily?" Victoria asked.

"Aunt Bella and I are going home to Black Manor. It'll be nice to just be us again and not teacher-student," Lily confessed, a small smile finding its way onto her face. That was something that Lily had seriously missed.

"That sounds fun for you." Sierra beamed.

Lily smiled. "I'm already excited."

"Uh-oh," Scotty said from his prized seat in the common room. He almost always had one of the two stand-alone chairs across from the couch that Lily, Amara, and Victoria claimed. Sierra would always claim the other stand-alone chair, pulled closer to the couch so Sierra could use the couch's armrest to help balance her books whenever she was taking notes. "Professor Black doesn't look happy."

Everyone turned, completely lacking any discretion, seeing several professors at the stairs, neutral expressions on their faces except for Bella, who was scowling furiously. She looked angrier than Lily had ever remembered seeing her in her life. Her onyx eyes were even darker as well. Based on how she looked, Lily guessed the Black family temper was barely restrained at that moment. It might be set off by anything.

"I wonder what happened," Victoria whispered.

"I don't know, but my aunt shouldn't be interrupted right now," Lily said as Sirius joined them and whispered something, making more professors scowl.

"I wonder what Professor Ryker said," Scotty mused aloud.

"The seventh years swear that they aren't involved and are scared," Amara said. When everyone looked at her, she smirked and shrugged. "Enhanced siren senses."

"Scared of what?" Sierra asked, alarmed.

"Probably Professor Black if they saw her."

Lily shot Scotty a dirty look for that comment. He at least had the decency to look sorry.

"Professor Snare is asking if any first year is capable or skilled enough to help in the breach," Amara supplied, still listening into the professors as they discussed the issue. She appeared to be acting casual, probably to not draw attention to herself or their friends.

"Breach?" Victoria asked nervously.

"Professor Black doubts it. She's more concerned with our safety as long as—" Amara snapped her mouth shut as she glanced at Victoria.

"As long as what?" Lily asked.

"As long as the ogre is loose on school grounds. Someone let it out of its cage."

Victoria squeaked at the mention of an ogre and paled considerably. Sierra and Scotty rubbed her back soothingly in response as Lily gazed at the professors again. They didn't seem alarmed, just tense…and mad.

"Happy Hallowe'en," Lily remarked dryly, mostly to herself.

"W-w-why is there an ogre here?" Victoria demanded, her voice an octave higher than normal.

"Maybe care of magical creatures and beasts?" Scotty supplied.

That was a fair conclusion.

"Ogres are class 3 designation, so if it is, it would be for fifth years and up," Sierra stated.

"Well…maybe it was captured coming onto school grounds, and they were waiting for it to be removed by the proper authorities?" Scotty suggested next.

"The closest location where ogres are naturally found is the Appalachian Mountains or the Rocky Mountains, since the North American ogres share the same territory as trolls. Or in the high north of Canada. Most ogres are in Europe or Asia though. Their population is extremely low, however, due to habitat loss," Sierra reported in a small lecture.

Victoria was quickly transitioning into a panic attack. All of them spent the next ten minutes calming her down, pulling her back from the brink, ignoring the professors. By the time she was calm again, Victoria looked exhausted. Fear does tend to take a lot out of a person. Lily, Sierra, and Amara guided Victoria to their room as Scotty waited on the couch for the three of them to return. By this point in the night, hardly anyone had left the common room, too curious as to why professors were hovering around.

Upon reaching their room, Lily turned the door handle, opened their door, and froze as a collective gasp came from their foursome. There, in their room, was the ugliest ogre Lily had ever seen (and she hadn't seen that many). It was easily eight feet high, probably closer to nine, and extremely fat. There was a scar across its right eye from an injury that had blinded it and a giant spiked club in its left hand. Its skin and big ears were a disgusting vomit-colored green, and the smell of it…Lily couldn't find anything remotely close to compare it to—it was that bad. They'd have to bleach their room for sure.

Maybe twice.

OK, three times.

Perhaps it would just be easier to burn the room down and build new. They could worry about that aspect later, once the ogre was removed from their room. The only clothing it had on—and Lily was being generous with the term *clothing*—was a ratty old loincloth that didn't look big enough to properly cover the ogre. On its feet were what looked like old animal hides that had been stitched together.

Just as Lily finished her astonished visual assessment, the ogre looked right at them and released a feral growl. The spiked club rose, and it took a single step toward the door in a threatening manner. That was where Lily drew the line.

"Wrong room. Run!" she cried and slammed the door shut again.

Victoria, at that most inopportune moment, fainted. Sierra and Amara caught her before she hit the floor, but it also trapped them for a few precious seconds at the one door that they shouldn't be anywhere near at that moment.

Together, the three dragged/carried Victoria away just as the door exploded behind them in a shower of wood chips, the spiked club sticking out of the newly formed hole. Picking up their pace considerably, they made a sprint (as best they could carrying Victoria) back to the common room. But luck was not on their side that day. Lily yelped as she was suddenly lifted off the ground like she weighed nothing. She watched her friends keep going, pause in shock, look back in horror, and then glance at the common room doors. They didn't know what they should do. Help her or go for safety…and help.

"Run!" Lily ordered. She then curled herself up, barely avoiding the club that the ogre swung at her. She never dreamed of becoming a piñata on Hallowe'en to some ugly ogre that managed to find its way into her room. Her friends remained frozen where they were, cradling Victoria and staring in horror at Lily. Another swing of the club, and

Lily twisted her body. It missed again…but brushed her hair. It was clear that none of them could do anything to stop this ogre, so that meant that they needed outside help to solve this issue. Lily knew that there was no way she could avoid the next swing.

"*Aunt Bella*!" Lily screamed at the top of her lungs, panic clear even to herself. This was her only hope at this point. She watched as the club came at her again before it bounced off of an invisible shield a foot from her to the ogre's confused grunt.

A blue spell struck the ogre in the upper chest, causing it to fall backward and release Lily as it lay there unmoving. Getting up from the floor, Lily looked to see Sirius and Bella with their wands raised. Bella sprinted for Lily, doing a quick damage check before she hugged her tightly in relief. Lily latched on to her and refused to let go as the adrenaline faded from her system.

"You're OK…You're OK," Bella cooed reassuringly.

She was no longer a professor at that moment; she was Lily's guardian. It took a couple of seconds for Lily to register that she was shaking and a few more still to realize tears were pouring down her cheeks unendingly.

"You girls are extremely lucky," Sirius said, helping Victoria to sit up and blocking most of her view of the ogre. "Not many can meet a mature Siberian mountain ogre unarmed and live to tell about the experience."

"I feel woozy," Victoria moaned, far too pale to be healthy.

"Let's get you to the infirmary," Sirius said as the other professors arrived and began to handle the now unconscious ogre, which was moaning a little now.

"C'mon, Lily. You can sleep with me tonight," Bella said.

Lily nodded rapidly against her chest. After that whole episode, she wasn't about to let Bella go just yet—not for several hours at the very least. She needed some serious comfort and a room that didn't play host for a terrifying ogre.

"I'd like a refund for this Hallowe'en," Lily remarked in a watery voice.

Bella chuckled and stroked Lily's black ringlet curls.

"I know the feeling, Lils."

CHAPTER VIII
UNEXPECTED CLUE

After the terrible excitement of Hallowe'en night, things remained calm and normal for Lily until Christmas. She had rejoined her still-shaken friends in their heavily cleansed room the next night and acted as though they hadn't almost just been killed. Scotty and Amara, however, were being more protective of them and hanging closer to them than what would be considered normal. But by Christmas break, they had all relaxed again and felt safe. Even Bella was no longer hovering around Lily when she was alone, which Lily admitted to missing. Now with it being Christmas though, Lily had Bella all to herself for the next two weeks, and she was going to take full advantage of the now very rare opportunity.

Back at Black Manor, a couple of inches of newly fallen pure-white snow covered the mansion and expansive grounds, and it was continuing to fall as Bella and Lily arrived in the foyer via apparition. It was amazing how comforting being home was and how both women instantly relaxed. The lobby was by far one of the more impressive areas of the manor as Lily removed her overcloak and handed her suitcase to one of the elves that appeared before her.

In the center of the lobby was a seven-foot tall, and probably six feet wide fountain with a statue of a wizard, wand pointed skyward with water spraying out of the tip stood proudly in the center. Behind the fountain, at the back of the lobby by the doorway that led to the main parlor, was the elaborate grand staircase that curled around the right side of the lobby to a walkway that was over the doorway leading to the other side of the second floor. They smiled at one another as they made their way from the lobby into the living room, where a large bare evergreen tree was awaiting them.

It had been tradition ever since Lily could remember that as soon as Bella came back to the manor for Christmas break, they'd spend the first day decorating the tree together, not using magic (except to put the star on top) and having fun. The small army of servant elves that the Black family employed kept everything inside as flawless and dust free in their absence as they did when they were there.

"Now, do you want to start with the lights or the ornaments?" Bella asked as several of the elves appeared with smiles on their faces, carrying boxes of decorations.

"Mmm…lights," Lily decided.

For the next hour, the two women decorated the tree (and each other while laughing) as the elves all decorated the extravagant manor around them for the holidays. Lily was so used to the opulence and regal ambience of the manor that she didn't give it another thought. But she was still able to appreciate that others coming in would be amazed by the sheer amount of wealth that was on display. After all, the Black family was very ancient, had a lot of old money, and earned millions of credits every year off of patents and royalties that they held. They had money to burn—literally. They could never spend it all. Probably Lily's grandchildren couldn't spend it all. Yeah, the Blacks were that rich.

Marble pillars, gold picture frames, lavishly carved exotic-wood furniture and staircases, silver utensils and dishware, and statues of family members from throughout the years (some of them only as busts) were spread throughout the manor, then there was a gorgeous full-sized indoor fountain in the lobby area. It was something to see. Lily was pulled from her musings suddenly as Bella wrapped her in a hug from behind and showered her face in kisses to Lily's giggles and delight.

"I'm very proud of you, Lily," Bella said, making Lily melt backward into her. She had no idea just how much that statement meant to Lily. It was one that she had secretly wanted to hear since the beginning of the school year.

"Thank you. It means a lot," Lily replied.

One last kiss to her cheek and Bella let her go. She pulled out her wand and levitated the star up into place at the top of the tree.

"Now, I'm in the mood for some hot chocolate. How about you?" Bella asked, getting an eager nod from Lily in return. So far, this break was looking very promising.

(☆)

FROM THEN UNTIL CHRISTMAS Day arrived, Lily and Bella hardly got out of their pajamas unless they absolutely had to. They watched nonmagical Christmas movies on the TV they had specifically for this reason, glommed together on the couch under a ridiculous amount of fluffy blankets; played games; or had the occasional all-too-serious snowball fight. But this morning, things were different. Bella had permitted Lily to sleep in her king-size bed with her on Christmas Eve, so they had woken up cuddling. After four failed attempts, they finally succeeded in hauling themselves from bed and headed downstairs to the tree, where their gifts were collected in a heap.

Lily brought hers and Bella's out, leaving the ones for their friends underneath to hand out when they returned to Gerhardt since there hadn't been—for once—a Christmas Eve party at Black Manor. Sirius was coming over, however, later in the day as had been the tradition. Christmas just wouldn't be complete without his presence.

Once the gifts were handed out, Bella sat down cross-legged on the floor across from Lily in her black silk pajama shirt and pants. Lily wore her own blue pajama set that accentuated her eyes. Bella opened her presents first: a couple new corsets, a new magical fiction book, a small night-table clock that Lily had transfigured in class from a small piece of wood (although it didn't work), and finally a black fox charm necklace. That one she had actually found at Gerhardt in the village when Bella had taken her there one weekend for a new dress to wear for the holidays. Then they found out that the party wasn't happening.

"It's beautiful, Lily," Bella crooned happily and put the necklace on immediately. "Your turn."

Lily looked at her presents and chose the biggest one to open first. After tearing open the wrapping, she popped the lid off the box and saw four brand-new corsets lying inside—two black of differing sizes, one dark green, and one navy blue. Lily looked up at her aunt, who was smiling like the cat that ate the canary. Lily highly suspected that there was some *lectio animo* involved in this.

"You promised not to read my mind," Lily accused, narrowing her eyes.

"I couldn't help but peek when you were eyeing the blue one, and the others are for your annual Hallowe'en costume. You'll soon outgrow your current one, so I was getting ahead of the curve," Bella replied.

Lily rolled her eyes and set them aside, but a smirk played at her lips.

The next present she grabbed was clearly a book of some sort. Unwrapping it, she was indeed greeted by a book. It was on all the known history of sirens—with a bolded warning on the cover that said it was nowhere near complete because of the serious lack of cooperation on the matter. Lily smiled at it and vowed to herself to read this one completely before they returned to Gerhardt at the end of the break. The one after that was a small ring box that made her look at Bella. The older woman was eyeing Lily in return with nervous interest.

"What's this?" Lily asked, lifting the box up a little more.

"It was your mother's. I bought it for her my sixth year at Gerhardt for her birthday. I think she would have wanted you to have it."

Flipping open the box, Lily gasped at the ring inside. It was solid gold and looked extravagant. The sides of the ring bore detailed engravings of lilies. Lilies were engraved upon the sides of the ring with lots of detail. On top was a beautiful ruby that was inlaid with the Black family motto around the stone: "Fidelis usque in sempiternum" (forever faithful). Around the circle of the motto were diamonds that drifted down into the engraved lilies. It was breathtaking. Bella smiled at Lily's reaction and gently lifted her chin to look at her.

"You have all of your mother's jewelry in your vault in a special case, whenever you want it. But this ring...I wanted to gift it to you, like I gifted it to my sister. That right there is the first thing I ever bought out of love for someone. I think that's why she gave it back to me that night when I last saw..." Bella stopped talking. Her eyes unfocused as she saw something that wasn't there. It happened only when she was thinking about Lily's mother Callista.

"Aunt Bella?" Lily asked, snapping Bella out of her trance.

"I did one tiny thing to the ring that it didn't have before. Press your finger against the ruby."

Lily did as she was asked and watched as a duplicate of the ring popped out into her hand. Examining this other ring and comparing the two together, Lily looked for any differences but found none. She then placed her finger over the ruby on the second one, but nothing happened. Confused, she looked back at Bella, who was bouncing happily with a big smile on her face. You would have thought that she was the kid and not Lily.

"I don't understand. How—"

"I enchanted the ring with a duplication charm that works only with the touch of a Black. The duplicate rings don't have that charm on them as a result. I really wasn't sure if I did it right, since this particular enchantment is pretty complex to use, but there was no way that I was going to ask Bloodstone to help me. I'd never hear the end of it!"

"But…why?"

"Lily…your friend hasn't had her normal diet," Bella said simply, trying to hint it to her.

Lily's brain kicked itself for not realizing it immediately.

"Amara can now have her version of chocolate!" Lily squealed in excitement with a face-splitting smile and hugged Bella before slipping the ring on her right-hand middle finger. It was a little loose, but she could make it work. Bella laughed as she handed Lily her next present.

It was a medium-sized box, but based on how it was lying, she guessed it was some sort of clothing article. After tearing apart the wrapping, she wasn't disappointed. Inside was a set of Bella's black dresses of various sizes. Another Halloween costume preparation. Well, on the bright side, at least she was set for the next few years. Her last present was another small one: a book about various types of historic artifacts in the magical world. Might be an interesting read, she supposed.

The fireplace flared up with pure white flames that seemed almost like fingers opening up around Sirius, who was now standing there with gifts under his arms and wiping some soot from his robes. Although that particular form of travel was considered the best and most reliable back in olden times, it was hardly ever used nowadays for two very good reasons. You got covered in soot, and you got so disoriented that you were incapacitated for several hours 80 percent of the time when you arrived at your destination. The British Magical Parliament used it liberally though, despite the thousands of grievances that they got from it on a monthly basis. Brits.

"Merry Christmas!" Sirius greeted, setting the presents he brought down. Then he smirked at Bella and the object that was hanging around her neck. "Nice necklace, Bella."

"Thank you. Lily got it for me." They shared a knowing smile before Bella narrowed her eyes accusingly at him. "You're early."

A look of innocence adorned Sirius's face.

"I am? My clock must need to be adjusted. Oh well, I'm here now, so I might as well stay."

Lily giggled as Bella's lips twitched.

"Fine, but you're helping the elves with breakfast," Bella ordered.

Sirius was now the one who scowled.

"That is cruel and unusual punishment. They're a well-oiled machine in there, and I'd just get in their way. Why would you torture them so?"

"Quit complaining, and get to cooking," Bella ordered.

Sirius glared at her before moving off to the kitchens with a handful of elves grumbling at the situation that they had just found themselves in.

❨ ☆ ❩

"Do you mind if I steal Bella for a couple minutes, Lily?" Sirius asked at the end of their rather lavish, if not a little subpar, breakfast.

Bella looked at him warily as Lily scowled at him. Her first real one-on-one time with her aunt since school started, and now she was being stolen away from her again? Even if it was just for a couple of minutes? Lily might just be a little possessive, but Bella was hers alone for this break.

"I'd prefer not," Lily replied.

"Even for a double chocolate hot cocoa with marshmallows?" Sirius smirked, raising an eyebrow.

Lily really hated the fact that he knew all of her weaknesses. Yet, based on the betrayed look Bella was giving him, it was clear her aunt also shared this particular weakness.

"The big ones or the small?" Lily asked.

"Small."

Bella's look became even more betrayed.

"Fine, two minutes tops…and Aunt Bella has to get one too," Lily stipulated.

Bella smiled smugly at Sirius, who playfully frowned but nodded in response. Black family for the win!

Once both women were handed their deliciously chocolatey drinks, Sirius and Bella left the room—the latter clutching her mug possessively. Lily savored the sinfully delicious drink as she played with the duplicate ring on her hand. By far, it was her favorite gift. She couldn't wait to show Amara this, certain her siren friend would be happily surprised. As she was busy contemplating the different reactions that Amara would have, Bella's hiss of a response immediately grabbed Lily's interest. Slinking quietly over to the door they were hidden behind, Lily listened in on whatever it was that had Bella so angry…and with Sirius of all people.

"Sirius, *no.*"

"Bella—"

"No means *no.*" There was a tense pause.

"Lily needs to be told, Bella."

"She's just a little girl, completely unprepared for this burden."

"So you want her to be blindsided?" Sirius accused. "Bella, none of this is a coincidence. That amulet being moved to Gerhardt from the vault in Drawlincott, the ogre on Hallowe'en night finding itself in Lily's room after it was deliberately released. The perimeter breaches to the school grounds have been happening since the first day of classes but seem to just be testing the wards—no signs of anyone having been there to try and breach them. It's *just* like before."

"Lily is safe," Bella insisted.

"She's *not* safe. Orion warns that she's going to be used by Sinestra, and I wholeheartedly agree. That amulet, if she gets it—"

"Your little ingenious solution makes it nearly impossible to be gotten. Completely from *her.*"

"We can't take any chances."

"Telling her will only hurt her," Bella stressed.

"What about not telling her? That will hurt her too since she'll think that you don't trust her," Sirius argued earnestly. Almost pleadingly.

"I do trust her, but she's better off not knowing. As long as the amulet is safe and away from Sinestra, then that's all that matters. Knowing will only weigh Lily down. She doesn't need that."

"I think she deserves to know. It's the right and smart thing to do. I think she can handle that truth." Sirius still fought.

"She's my responsibility; therefore, it's my decision," Bella said with finality.

Lily retreated back before she was caught eavesdropping and reclaimed her mug just as both professors exited the room, acting like they hadn't just fought. It was truly amazing how well they could hide their feelings when they wanted to. From there, the three engaged in small talk until Bella and Lily headed upstairs to finally get dressed for the day. Despite the topics of conversation, Lily's mind kept replaying the information that she had learned covertly.

The ogre incident was linked to other events that were suspicious. Sinestra was out there somewhere on the loose and wanted this mysterious amulet, and she was targeting Lily for…some reason. She wondered idly again why Sinestra was never locked away for killing her parents. Shouldn't that have been what happened? There had to be a reason why not. Lily made a mental note to look into it when she returned to Gerhardt. For the time being, she'd just enjoy the break while it lasted and before the stress of classes returned to her life.

CHAPTER IX
REVELATIONS

The moment Lily returned to Gerhardt, she made a beeline for her shared room and entered, tossing the duplicate ring at Amara, who caught it in her hand without looking up from the book she was reading. Only after she had finished her paragraph did she look at the ring and then at Lily, who was beaming at her excitedly. Amara examined the ring before she looked back at Lily for an explanation. When Lily didn't provide one, Amara set her book aside and turned her body to fully face her friend.

"Why toss me this ring?"

"You can eat it," Lily said matter-of-factly. Amara looked at the ring again and shook her head defiantly.

"No, Lily, this ring is far too nice for you to—"

"Look." Lily walked over to stand right beside the siren's bed and placed a finger over the ruby of the ring on her finger. Another duplicate popped out into her hand. She handed it to Amara. The siren stared at Lily in complete awe and perhaps even warmth.

"You're a special surface dweller, Lily. I don't know if I deserve your friendship."

"Yes, you do, Amara. And you're a pretty special siren too. Anything to make you feel more comfortable."

Amara stood up and hugged Lily, giving the Pureblood witch a sense of safety and warmth that she had only felt from Bella. Then there was the urge to bury her face in Amara's neck and forget about…ugh, siren scent. It was lovely, but Lily was really beginning to get annoyed by it messing with her. Amara pulled away and popped one of the rings into her mouth. She chewed it up to bits with no more effort than you would with a chocolate bar…maybe even less.

"That will definitely take some getting used to seeing," Victoria said from her bed, a rock in front of her. She was using it for her transfiguration practice like they had in charms class.

"Is Sierra back yet?" Lily asked, seeing her stuff gathered on her bed.

"Yeah, she arrived here just before you, She said she'd—" Victoria was cut off by the person in question as Sierra entered the room again in a slight huff.

"Next time I go home, I swear, I'm using the floo service, no matter the faults with it. That was the longest drive I've ever sat through— longer than to initially come here at the beginning of the school year! Winter driving is the *worst*!" Sierra vented.

Victoria and Amara looked at Sierra, confused.

"Drive?" Victoria questioned.

"It's…well…I'll explain it later. I'm not in the mood right now."

"Hey, Sierra, I need to pick your encyclopedic brain," Lily said, plopping herself down on the bookworm's bed to her scowl. "Have you ever read anything on Sinestra?"

"Some. Why?"

"Lily," Amara warned in a voice harder than Lily would have expected. "That topic shouldn't be discussed."

"Amara, she killed my parents. I want to know why she wasn't arrested for that, why she's still out there somewhere. Why did she manage to just vanish into thin air? Even by magical standards, that's impressive," Lily argued defensively.

"Which is understandable," the siren sympathized. "But she's one of the most evil dark witches of all time. Grandmother told me about her and her cause."

"Cause?" Lily asked, confused.

"She started the Unfinished War," Amara stated, causing Sierra to jump in.

"I read up about that. Her goal was to have magical folk rule over nonmagical people because magic makes us the superior group. She argued that to hide our abilities is against our nature. She also hates Nonbloods, although that is nothing more than speculation. But in terms of documentation, it was well documented that she wanted to wipe them out and enslave every nonmagical person. But the main draw she had was the forced eradication of the international secrecy laws."

"That's what made a lot of witches and wizards flock to her side, giving her the largest magical army of all time, spread out over North America and even some ocean folk. Grandma said she was even gaining a massive following in France, Germany, and Russia at the time of her mysterious disappearance on January 1, 2000."

"Huh?" Lily asked. She was getting somewhere now.

"She was at the height of her power and then just…vanished. Without her, her army faded back into the shadows. She was the only thing keeping the massive conglomerate together. That's why they call it the Unfinished War. Both sides fought for two years and were evenly matched until Sinestra vanished. The war was on the verge of massive escalation when she did vanish." Amara shrugged. "It's still a very sensitive topic all these…well, twelve years later."

"Mmm. Well, she's finally returned to finish it then," Lily said, pursing her lips.

Victoria straightened her back, eyes locked onto Lily.

"Why do you say that?" she asked nervously.

"Remember that ogre?"

"I try not to," Victoria confessed with a shiver.

"Well, I overheard—"

"Hey," a short-haired platinum blonde with a dyed aqua streak—Harmony Para—said in their doorway, "your guy friend is in the common room wanting to talk to you guys. He seems stressed."

"Thank you, Harm," Lily said, making the other girl smile wider.

She was a Halfblood that was actually a neighbor to Black Manor, just off of the massive property. Lily had taken a liking to her when she found that out, getting to meet one of her neighbors. Together the girls all headed out in a mass for the common room.

Waiting for them by the door, looking concerned and pacing anxiously, was Scotty. Lily didn't like seeing him in this state at all; it didn't suit him. As soon as he spotted them, he breathed a massive sigh of relief, his shoulders relaxing. Lily raised her eyebrow at him. He nodded toward the stairs. The girls following him in silence, their little band meandered through the halls to a relatively empty area. Once they were there, Scotty began talking.

"I feared that something bad happened to you guys. I've been freaking out for days now."

"Why?" Sierra asked.

"My mom was asked to assign some of the best Themida to the school by the Magical president and Professor Orion."

Themida? Assigning them to Gerhardt? Lily wasn't sure that she had ever heard of that happening before.

"Uh, Scotty, what does your mom do again?" Lily asked. She knew that Mrs. Halifax worked at the Congress, but she didn't recall ever knowing what it was exactly that she did there.

"She's the second in command of the Magical Law Enforcement Division. Normally she's the one who handles all things at the Magical Congress, like security, prisoner transfers from courts to prison, and the overall paperwork of the department."

"So that's who all the new faces are," Amara remarked.

"Why would Themida—top Themida at that—be sent here?" Victoria asked.

It was a good question. Themida weren't people that you necessarily wanted to cross if you were into the dark arts. They were the elite dark wizard hunters, law enforcement, and soldiers who would fight any war that might pop up. They were feared because they were relentless when they went after their prey. They specialized in dark arts studies in order to combat their opponents on even ground.

Lily cleared her throat pointedly, gaining their attention.

"I've got a hunch: Sinestra."

"Lily—" Amara said.

"Listen to me before you argue," Lily pleaded, raising her palms to her friends. "All year so far, there've been breaches to school grounds and the perimeter wards. That ogre in our room, Sirius doesn't think it's a coincidence. I overheard him and Aunt Bella talking about it over the break."

"But why?" Scotty asked, confused.

"There's an amulet that she wants. It was moved here, and she's trying to get it," Lily supplied.

"OK, but why?" Sierra asked, furrowing her brow. "All that makes sense, but what's the reason for it, and what's so special about this amulet?"

"I don't know. But it can't be anything good," Lily confessed.

"There can't be too many places here at the school to hide some precious amulet. I'm sure it's well guarded," Victoria said confidently. That was a fair statement. There weren't that many places that Lily had seen where an object could be hidden, and the spaces where it could would most likely have a bunch more wards in place for added security. But she just had a bad feeling surrounding that thought—like no matter what was in place, it might not be enough.

It was difficult, but Lily managed to find some old news articles referring to Sinestra and the beginning of her war. It gave a little insight into just how dangerous and charismatic Sinestra really was. The number of disappearances of those who opposed her or talked badly against her cause—or who were simply Nonbloods—was staggering. The numbers were almost hard to believe.

Her forces weren't just composed of ordinary witches and wizards either. There were plenty of ordinary folk, sure, but some of the worst dark witches and wizards who weren't afraid of using the forbidden curses were in her personal legions. The seediest of the magical world and the worst blood supremacists filled her ranks in addition to the common folk who believed Sinestra was the only person able to bring needed change. Their personal savior. The next Merlin. She had followers from every walk of life.

There was even a name given for her own most devout personal shock troops: Venatores Mortem—or death hunters. You get the idea off of their name as to what it was that they were like. They were the worst.

Some of these Venatores Mortem were arrested and sent to Xurban prison for their crimes after she vanished. But the hunt for the majority didn't get anywhere. Lily suspected several bribed their way out of trouble and others just took off and hid somewhere remote. Overall, that had led to a dead end in information. So, Lily turned her attention to researching the amulet with Sierra…and came up empty-handed other than living in the library for several weeks. There was nothing on a special amulet that they could find anywhere in Gerhardt's expansive library. All of this frustration was giving Lily a massive headache.

"Sorry, Lily. Looks like we've hit a dead end," Sierra apologized as they entered the common room again after their latest failure.

"Well, we gave it our all," Lily conceded sadly. It was the truth. They covered all the reading material they could (which given that the giant library had books and reading materials on literally every square inch of wall and tabletop was saying something) to find answers to their questions, but it wasn't enough.

Amara and Scotty were practicing some charms (OK, Amara was practicing; Scotty was struggling) at their usual couch as Lily and Sierra joined them with their books. Amara glanced at them, but Scotty just remained focused intently on his task. Lily was about to make a comment to him about his technique when the object he was trying to charm bounced onto the floor and shot right at Lily's face. She closed her eyes and waited for impact and the pain that she'd feel afterward…

but it never came. Only the sound of it hitting skin. It was moving way too fast for anyone to catch it, but…Lily opened her eyes and saw Amara's right fist in front of her face. There was no doubt that Amara had caught it. How fast *could* she move?

"Perhaps it's time for a break, yes?" Amara questioned.

Scotty nodded and looked apologetically toward Lily.

"You'll get the hang of it, Scotty," Sierra chimed in encouragingly. Lily nodded her agreement and smiled at him reassuringly.

"I don't understand why it's so hard for me to do these things," he lamented.

"Perhaps charms is just your weak area," Sierra supplied with a shrug.

"It's not just charms though!" he groaned.

Lily looked up from their positions on the couch and saw Nikki Nero walk down to the bottom of the stairs and look around. This was the first time that Lily had seen Nikki outside of her classroom or the grand mess. This immediately raised Lily's curiosity and interest.

It took a few moments, but Nikki's eyes finally met Lily's, causing a smile to form on the older woman's face. She gave a subtle nod up the stairs and then disappeared up them. Looking around, Lily thought no one else seemed to have noticed the teacher's presence in the room besides her. It seemed that her cousin wanted to talk with her privately. This could be exciting.

"I'll be right back," Lily said, getting to her feet. She headed off to the stairs and climbed up them quickly to find Nikki walking slowly along the walkway to the rest of the school. As soon as Lily appeared beside her, Nikki increased her pace to a more normal gait.

"How are you, Lily?" Nikki asked pleasantly.

"I'm fine, Professor. Just trying to keep up with all of the work we're being given."

"I remember." Nikki giggled. "Trust me, being a student is far easier than being a teacher. I have double or triple the workload you do."

"You chose it," Lily jested to Nikki's amused laugh. She smiled.

"More like I was asked to make this my challenge. I originally dreamed of being a Themida."

"Really?" Lily asked, shocked.

"Oh yeah." Nikki nodded. "I completed all of the needed course-work and scored in the top three of the new recruits. Many of the best Themida were interested in taking me on as their apprentice. But when Aunt Bella said that Professor Mercy was going to retire soon, and I'd get to work at Gerhardt, I had to jump at the offer. There's a waiting list to teach here, you know."

"But transfiguration?" Lily asked. It didn't exactly scream "Themida recruit here."

"I got an outstanding score in it and protections against the dark magical arts," Nikki said. "Surprisingly, Themida must have at least a perfect score to even qualify. If you're interested in that as a career in a few years, I'll tell you all about it," Nikki said, winking.

Lily smiled and nodded as they kept walking.

In a few years, she'd need to figure out what career she wanted. That just made her head spin. She could put that off for the time being, no need to get ahead of herself. She had time.

They walked together in companionable silence for a while just enjoying this newly discovered bond they had. It was nice having more family than just Bella in her life. Oh, by all means, Bella was all Lily really needed, but Nikki had something that Bella didn't: she had a sisterly feel. Bella was more of a motherly figure. Lily was finding it comforting to have a sort of older sister, someone she could go to for advice if Bella wasn't available.

"Professor?"

"Mhmm?"

"I have the feeling that this one-on-one time isn't just to check in on my academic progress out of familial concern…is it?" Lily knew questioning this was a bit of a risk, but her gut was telling her this was connected to the events happening around them. Asking this question was going to eliminate the easygoing camaraderie they had, she was sure, but she needed some answers. Nikki hesitated and then sighed.

"You're definitely just as clever as Aunt Bella. No, I wanted to make sure you're safe."

"Themidas are at the school, I have all the professors around me like bodyguards, and I have my friends; I'm fine."

"I understand your exasperation, Lily, but the ogre incident says otherwise," Nikki warned.

"I'm no damsel in distress," Lily growled. This was getting very annoying.

"Never said you were. But you are just a first-year student."

"Is it really just because of that and that I'm learning just the bare basics at the moment or that Sinestra has me firmly in her crosshairs?"

Oh, Lily hadn't meant to say that.

Nikki stopped walking and stared at Lily with an unreadable expression. Lily decided—since she'd already inadvertently spilled the beans—to take a chance. "Is my hunch correct? Is she after me? I know she's out there somewhere."

Nikki turned her body to look out a nearby window, crossing her arms over her chest. Her purple hair was shifting to different colors as she contemplated her response. She must be a morphmagi—someone who could change their physical appearance (and sometimes their voice too) at their own will. It was a very rare trait to be born with but highly prized. A Themida morphmagi would be legendary. A dark witch or wizard with that gift would be very dangerous. When Nikki's hair returned to its "normal" purple color, she looked back at Lily.

"You're correct. But she's *not* going to get you. All of us refuse to let that happen. Just…don't do anything foolish or risky, OK?"

"So, nothing that the Black family is known for."

Nikki smirked in amusement. "Pretty much."

"No promises," Lily said playfully.

"You do something you shouldn't, and Aunt Bella will have your head," Nikki warned.

"I know. But she has a soft spot for me."

Nikki laughed, shaking her head as she wrapped an arm around Lily's shoulders. That playful feeling had returned.

"That's more than I have with her. Consider yourself lucky."

"Sirius said the same thing to me when I was little."

Nikki laughed even louder.

With that, they turned around and headed back for the dorms. Lily had learned some very valuable information about Nikki from their conversation, and she had gotten confirmation that she was Sinestra's other target. But that amulet…A horrifying thought struck her. Sinestra was targeting her as a distraction to get that amulet. She had to tell her friends about this. Things were finally beginning to come together and make sense.

(☆)

"THAT DOES MAKE A lot of sense. She killed your parents, then vanished. In order to get this amulet, she'll target you to make everyone think she wants to finish what she started. Then, as everyone's focus is on you, the amulet disappears with her," Scotty deduced, pacing in front of the couch Lily and the rest of her friends were sitting on. It was a bit squished.

"Then Lily's in danger," Victoria said, looking at Lily with a mild alarm.

"We should tell the professors," Sierra cautioned.

"And have me be watched even more than I am right now? No, thanks!" Lily spat.

"That would be the better option than losing you," Amara said, her eyes pleading.

Lily stood and paced with Scotty for several moments. She didn't want to be watched more closely. At the same time, she really didn't want to let Amara down at all. The mere thought of leaving Amara—and her other friends—behind if something happened to her was making her heart ache way too much. There had to be a middle ground somewhere.

"We need to find that amulet," Lily declared at last.

Scotty whipped around to face her.

"No, we shouldn't. The professors can handle guarding it with the Themida. That's what they're here for."

"Lily, protecting the amulet isn't your responsibility," Sierra stressed. "Focus on what's best for you. That means staying safe and protected."

Some part of Lily's brain wanted to keep arguing. She wanted to prevent Sinestra from getting that amulet. But the majority of her brain knew that she shouldn't. Bella would be devastated if anything happened to her, and Lily didn't want to stress her out. After that ogre incident, she wanted Bella to have a less stressful job of worrying about her.

Besides, thinking realistically, what good could a first-year student really do against a witch like Sinestra—the most powerful dark witch of her time and perhaps all time? It would be like trying to put out a house fire with a squirt gun. Not very effective. There would only be one end result, and Lily really didn't want to think about that right now. Sighing in defeat, she collapsed back onto the couch with her friends.

"If this is what prison feels like, then I want nothing to do with any prison."

"If feeling like you're in a prison keeps you safe, then it's worth it," Amara countered.

"It's annoying."

"Only to you. Can't you see that this is for the best?" Sierra asked.

Lily snorted, making all of them roll their eyes. "Real mature, Lily."

"Let me pout in peace, Sierra."

CHAPTER X
WATER VAULT

Of all the classes that they had, potions was arguably the most mixed in terms of student interest. In their lives, potions were vital and a foundation of magic. That was why it was considered a core class for all seven years. That being said, 99 percent of all potions were complex and required genuine skill to master. Professor Snare was arguably one of the best potion masters there was…even if his grouchy personality turned students off of him. Then again, he might be grouchy because he was the only teacher—and classroom in the entire school—who was in the basement. Most of the rest of the basement was the teachers' living quarters and storage. A lot of rooms and musty odor.

Unlike the rest of the classrooms, and the rest of the basement for that matter, the potions classroom had no natural light inside. Well, that wasn't entirely true. There was one half-moon window of stained glass above and behind Snare's desk, but the light that was coming through it was so minimal that it was almost nonexistent. The entire room was lit therefore by a plethora of candles and wall-mounted torches.

Lily had a hard time stomaching the fumes from her cauldron at times because of improper ventilation.

Amara looked worse, thanks to a small explosion of toxic-smelling smoke that flew directly in her face. She actually looked like she was going to throw up. As Lily added the final ingredient, their potion of nyerwart turned a pale-blue color, signaling that they had done it right. Once Snare had come over, checked them off, and dismissed them, both girls made a beeline for the doorway with their belongings in search of the promise of clean air.

"You OK, Amara?" Lily asked, concerned, as Amara swallowed hard.

"I just may prove sirens *can* vomit," she returned, making Lily giggle.

According to her book, that was something that sirens had said was impossible.

"You're looking better though."

They stood there in the hallway for a couple minutes as Amara breathed.

"I'm now feeling better," Amara said, looking normal again. "No vomiting. Must be true after all."

Lily laughed louder, making Amara smile. But as they walked further toward the main stairs to head up to the ground floor, Amara stopped and looked down a small corridor that Lily had never noticed before. Had it always been there? Why hadn't she seen it then? She wasn't *blind*. The redheaded siren stared down it, making Lily glance between her and the corridor.

"Amara?"

"There's water down there. Enchanted water."

"Enchanted?"

"From Atlantis's Poseidon Bank Vaults. It has a very unique feel and presence."

"Huh?" Lily was so confused.

"Water that prevents surface dwellers from entering," Amara explained. "Unlike other enchanted waters, this is done by the ocean. It's naturally enchanted and has added magic from magical creatures."

"Are you saying that we can enchant water?"

"No. Only members of the ocean can. You can bend it, control it to a minimal degree. But not enchant."

"Oh." Lily furrowed her brows. "So why is your enchanted water here? And what's so special—"

"Enchanted water, as I said, keeps surface dwellers out. You can't breathe in it with magic charms or potions or plants. It also nullifies most magic from residents of the ocean. Perfect for bank vaults," Amara said quickly. "As for why it's here…I don't know. The Siren Sword isn't in it."

Lily gazed down the corridor, trying to piece this puzzle together. Why have enchanted water at Gerhardt? In all the times they'd walked to and from potions, Amara hadn't once stopped like this, so it had to be new. Then again, there was no way that this corridor was constructed overnight—even with magic. It also looked as old as the rest of the basement, and that couldn't be faked. It must've had protective wards hiding it. What could possibly need protective wards in the school? The siren sword wouldn't, so what…Wait a minute.

"This is where the amulet is being housed!" Lily said excitedly.

"Then we'd better leave," Amara said, shoving Lily toward the stairs.

Lily peered at the corridor a few more seconds before she lost it thanks to Amara's pushing.

"This is huge, Amara!"

"You aren't going after it."

"But—"

"No."

"Oh c'mon!" Lily whined. She crossed her arms over her chest as Amara spun her 180 degrees, placed her hand between Lily's shoulder blades, and gently pushed. It was either walk against this force or fall down flat on her face. Lily begrudgingly chose to walk.

"This isn't our place to interfere. It is well protected."

"Party pooper."

Amara paused in her pushing.

"Who would bring fecal matter to a party?"

Lily bellowed out in laughter, leaving Amara even more confused. Once Lily was able to breathe again, and her tears of laughter were wiped away, she explained, "No, 'party pooper' refers to someone who kills fun for others. I'm saying you're no fun right now."

"Oh…That makes a lot more sense," Amara conceded. Then she resumed pushing on Lily's back. It was clear that this day, Lily had lost the battle.

"You can stop pushing now. We're far enough away," Lily weakly protested. The small contact she had had with Amara was soothing to her. She kind of wished that she hadn't said anything now.

"Very well." Amara removed her hand and walked beside Lily as they headed to the common room.

❨ ☆ ❩

A MERE TWO DAYS later, Lily was still thinking about the accidental discovery that she and Amara had made. She had a gut feeling that the amulet wasn't safe despite the enchanted water. Her friends, naturally, disagreed. They wanted to have her forget this entire thing and focus on other things—like living in the library with Sierra or helping Scotty get a grip on their schoolwork. But as Lily lay on her bed reading her siren book again a little before curfew, a knock came at their closed door. All four girls looked at it in confusion since a closed door—particularly this late in the evening—meant the occupants didn't want to be disturbed. Another, more forceful knock sounded before the door opened, revealing a distressed-looking Bella whose expression then morphed into one of relief. Lily placed a bookmark in her book, as Bella's hand relaxed on the handle.

"You're OK."

"Yes…why, Aunt Bella?" Lily asked, sitting up and setting her book aside.

"Just a feeling I had. Nothing to worry about. Good night, girls," Bella said and left, closing the door behind her. As soon as it latched, Lily's friends looked at her.

"I bet it has to do with the amulet," Lily said with conviction.

"Um…playing devil's advocate," Victoria piped up, "Lily having all this attention on her is keeping her safe. Perhaps safer than some special mystical water."

"Are you saying we go and steal it?" Sierra squeaked. "That's breaking so many rules! We'll get in trouble! We could get expelled! Oh, oh boy…expelled…" Sierra looked pale.

"I disagree. The enchanted water can protect it." Amara spoke up.

"We're at a stalemate. We have Scotty as the tiebreaker," Lily said, jumping out of bed and dashing out of the room.

"Lily, wait!" Sierra yelled. By the time the other three girls had reached her, Lily was in the common room and had stopped Scotty from entering the boy dorms.

"Scotty! Do we go and get the amulet or not?" Lily demanded quickly before she was stopped.

He blinked back at her tiredly. "You found it?"

Oh, yeah, they hadn't told him that yet. There was a distinct disadvantage to him being a boy when the rest of them were girls. They seriously needed to come up with a solution to that problem.

"Scotty, say no. Lily's lost her mind," Sierra pleaded.

"Does this have anything to do with Professor Black showing up here in a rush?" Scotty asked, raising an eyebrow.

"Yes. Answer please," Lily demanded.

He smiled at her. "I say let's go! A little adventure never hurt nobody."

"I've become the only sane one left," Sierra muttered.

Lily ignored her and led her little band of friends out of the dorms and toward the corridor. It was exciting, doing something that they shouldn't, and based on the smirks that everyone was wearing—even Sierra, though she was trying to hide it—they were thinking the same thing. They were alert for any teachers who were in the halls though. There was no need to take unnecessary risks.

Upon reaching the corridor, Amara led the way and brought them all to the last room at the end. The amulet was on the other side. Lily would bet on it. Once they'd picked the lock (going through half a dozen iterations of the spell before Sierra finally got fed up and did it properly with a protest), they entered together and gasped.

Right in front of them was a gigantic pool—easily twenty feet long and fifteen feet wide with a maximum depth of about thirty feet. On the bottom was a beautiful tile mosaic of water creatures that, at Amara's presence, moved about happily. Lily also noticed that when Amara neared the water glowed a light-aqua color. The water inside the pool was crystal clear and as smooth as glass. Almost too clear, Lily mused. Down on the deep bottom—around fifteen feet down—in the exact center of the pool was the amulet placed on a stone positioned there.

"Since when did Gerhardt have a giant pool?" Victoria asked.

"It was put in in 1973 for the seventh years. It was used until 1995 when it became too sparsely used. It clearly now serves a new purpose," Sierra reported.

"I'd use it daily," Lily remarked, kneeling at the edge.

"So would I," Amara said and smiled.

"OK, so how do we get it?" Scotty asked, hands perched on his hips. Lily shrugged.

"Simple. Amara's the only one who can breathe in this water, so her."

"I cannot touch it," Amara said, frowning.

"The water? You're a siren! You live in it!" Scotty cried in shock.

"Not the water, the amulet. The runes prevent me."

"Runes?" Lily looked closer and saw there was something carved into it, but she couldn't make it out. It was too small for her to really see.

"They're antimagical creature runes. Very ancient."

"Well, we can't get it. We tried. Let's go back to bed before we're caught out after curfew," Sierra said, turning for the door. Lily stood and placed her hands on her hips with a determined scowl. It would take more than some runes against magical creatures to stop her from getting it.

"We have to get it."

"Well…" Amara began playing with her fingers. "There is one trick I know that could make you breathe underwater, Lily. My mother's done it a couple of times with some of her victims."

"You aren't going to kill her, right?" Victoria asked nervously.

"No!" Amara panicked. "No, it…forget it."

"Amara, I trust you completely. If it will allow me to get that amulet, do whatever you have to," Lily reassured her quickly.

Amara looked touched and required a few seconds to regain her composure. Once she had, she stepped into Lily's personal space and held her hands up pleadingly.

"Promise not to freak out?"

"I promise," Lily vowed as Amara gently moved her black ringlet curls away from the left side of her neck.

Lily wasn't entirely sure what she should expect, but she had meant it with her entire heart when she said she trusted Amara completely. She also meant it when she promised not to freak out. However, that was harder to obey than she thought when Amara's teeth penetrated her neck. Then she and Lily were underwater a second later. Lily gasped. She expected to swallow water and did, but it didn't enter her lungs. It seemed that the water vanished at her throat, and air replaced it—right where Amara's teeth and mouth were.

"Amara, are you doing this?" Lily asked. She sounded exactly like she did when she talked in the air.

"Mhmm," Amara hummed against her neck. Oh…Lily had a new favorite sensation. That was when Lily noticed the next incredible thing.

Amara was moving through the water like it was air. It was eerie and yet cool to see at the same time. Within seconds, they were at the amulet, and Amara turned them so Lily could see and reach for it.

Stretching out, Lily grabbed it, signaled Amara a bit reluctantly, and then shot to the surface faster than any human could have managed. She found herself getting laid out on the edge before Amara's teeth left her neck and her tongue licked the crescent wounds. Lily was soaked, but Amara—still in the water to her chest—looked completely dry… minus her soaked clothes. Gingerly touching her neck, Lily found the wounds completely gone, like they'd never been there to begin with.

"How…" Lily asked, speechless.

"Siren saliva has immense healing properties. More so than phoenix tears and saliva actually," Amara replied, shrugging. It was then that Lily noticed there were no ripples from Amara in the water, like she wasn't even there.

"We have a lot to learn about you, Amara," Victoria said in awe.

"Can one of you transfigure a towel please?" Lily asked, sitting up.

"I'll do one better," Sierra said, pulling out her wand. "*Evaporo!*"

Steam rose from Lily's clothes as they dried, and her hair lost its held water too. Amara leaped out and got the same treatment from Sierra. Now with dry clothes and with the amulet secure in Lily's hands, they sneaked back to their common room.

All of them then peeled off to their individual beds, deciding that the amulet could be examined in the morning. The day had been long enough as it was, and they needed to be fresh to work through this mystery. After setting the amulet aside on her nightstand, Lily stared at it in the moonlit room until sleep finally overtook her. She had the amulet. That was the hard part.

"LILY?"

With great effort, Lily pried open her eyes, which were still heavy with sleep to see Sierra leaning over her. Sunlight was filtering into the room, illuminating it and showing Victoria dressed as Amara put on her overcloak.

"Did I sleep in?" Lily moaned.

"Slept like the dead. I've been trying to wake you for five minutes," Sierra confessed anxiously. Lily sat up and began a hurried dressing before shoving the amulet into her overcloak pocket with a yawn. This was going to be a long day.

Sure enough, throughout the day, Lily only got progressively more tired, and by the time she got to protections against the dark magical arts, she was nearly asleep in her seat. If Amara hadn't gently elbowed her twice, she would have fallen asleep—and likely received Aunt Bella's wrath. Just as class wrapped up, Bella did come over and lightly laid her hand on Lily's shoulder. She lifted her head off of her hand sleepily to see Bella kneeling beside her desk. Of course she'd ask about this.

"Lily, are you OK?" Bella asked.

"Yeah. Just didn't sleep well yesterday."

Bella's eyes softened. "Well, get a good night's sleep tonight. I'm sure your friends will make sure of that anyway, but you do look awful, Lils."

"I feel awful too. All I want right now is to sleep," Lily confessed.

"Then go. To. Bed," Sirius said from the doorway of his office, which was normal stone today, no transparency. He was even looking at her with mild concern.

"C'mon, Lily," Amara urged, gently pulling her arm.

"OK, OK, I'm coming. Let me—" All her books and supplies floated into her bag, nullifying her need to pack. "Never mind."

"I'll carry it," Victoria offered.

Lily handed it to her without a fight and in the middle of a yawn. Then she basically let her friends lead her back to her room.

Once inside, she collapsed face-first onto her bed and groaned into the mattress. It felt like her bones were filled with lead; she was that tired. She'd never in her life felt like this before. Could…could it be the amulet? With the last of her rationed energy, Lily pulled the amulet out and dropped it to the floor. As soon as it was a little away from her, she felt minutely better. There was definitely a connection of some sort.

"Ouch!" Sierra yelped.

Lily forced her head up to see the pads of two fingers on Sierra's right hand bright red from a burn.

"How did—" Lily began, but Amara interrupted her.

"The runes. Only Purebloods can touch it."

"Here," Victoria said, bending down. She picked it up as everyone began to speak warnings of the stupidity of her act to her. But they all died in their throats when Victoria straightened with the amulet in her hand, safe and sound. She eyed it for a few seconds, studying it, before she looked at their shocked expressions.

"You're a Pureblood?" Sierra asked, still cradling her hand.

"Yeah…I didn't tell you guys, did I?" Victoria confessed timidly and shrank a little into herself. A small blush began to color her cheeks. "Sorry."

"That's OK," Lily said, dropping her head again. "We understand it slipping your mind. Particularly when we don't care about what our individual blood status is."

"Well, Lily, you sleep. We'll have Victoria hold on to the amulet tonight," Amara said.

Lily moaned before her exhaustion finally took over.

CHAPTER XI
THE AMULET

Lily awoke late the next morning but felt refreshed, like she normally was after sleeping instead of the sheer exhaustion from the previous day. Looking around, she saw Victoria and Amara sitting on Victoria's bed with the amulet between them on the blanket. They were quietly discussing the latest potions essay and which parts they were finding difficult. Sierra was absent—most likely holed away in the library—leaving the room emptier than Lily was used to feeling it.

It was astonishing how much her friends meant to her now. To a degree, they'd quickly become like a family. Lily's heart warmed immensely at that thought. Her aunt was right. She did need friends. Amara looked at her and smiled at that moment.

"How're you feeling, Lily?" she asked.

"Better," Lily confessed. "What have I missed?"

"Not much," Victoria confessed with a shrug. "Sierra drafted Scotty to research the runes on this while we guard it and you."

Them? Guard her? Lily dropped that thought as irritation began to enter her mind.

"How long have they been gone?" Lily asked, sitting up.

"All morning," Victoria replied.

"Mmm," Lily hummed. "Were you suddenly tired after touching that, Vic?"

"No." Victoria smiled at the nickname and shrugged. "I felt—and still feel—fine."

"It might be a side effect of me. I'm sorry," Amara confessed, looking a little guilty.

That was another possibility. Lily stood, stretched satisfyingly, used the bathroom, and then walked over to Victoria's bed. Sitting beside the two redheads, she eyed the amulet again.

It was bigger than she had expected but easily fit into the palm of a hand. A stone of polished obsidian was inlaid in the center of the silver amulet. The runes that prevented anyone but a Pureblood from touching it were engraved around the outermost edge on a gold ring. Despite the ancient nature of the runes, the amulet itself looked nearly brand new. This mystery was just getting more and more confusing. Why would Sinestra want this thing? Nothing was adding up.

"Hey, Sleeping Beauty finally woke up!" Sierra said, opening the door a few seconds later.

"Yeah…Sleeping Beauty?" Lily questioned, making Sierra sigh.

"It's a nonmagical movie. I'll show you guys it one day."

"All right," Lily said and then refocused on the present. "What did you find?"

"Nothing! Absolutely nothing!" Sierra huffed, slamming the door behind her in frustration. "Nowhere in Gerhardt's extensive and heavenly library are there any materials matching those ancient runes or anything close to resembling them! The ones that are in the library aren't even classified as ancient!"

"What do you mean?" Victoria asked, confused.

"The 'ancient' classification when it comes to magic is any magical thing that was created before the Hyperkasen Cataclysm, circa AD 100. After the Cataclysm, magic changed to what we have today. It had become—as rumored by texts—less powerful."

"So these runes date back to at least AD 100," Lily surmised after Sierra finished her brief lecture.

"Far older. My grandmother developed an interest in ancient magic—mainly runes—from Professor Ryker. She's taught me a little about them throughout the years. It's at least from 730 BC. They're also slightly modified from the original. Specialized, you might say," Amara supplied.

"You are just full of surprises!" Sierra scoffed. "I did discover something else though."

"Oh?" Lily asked, intrigued.

"Over the next few weeks, we'll be getting a bunch of package deliveries from home!"

That was a really special treat! Normally, the first and second years didn't get packages except at the beginning of the year and right before exams. The rule was to keep them focused. They must have been exceptionally good.

"I'm not expecting anything to come for me," Amara said, shrugging. "My mother would never, and Grandmother will only send letters."

"I'm not going to get anything either," Victoria whispered.

"That makes three of us striking out then. With Aunt Bella being here, there isn't really anyone to send me anything," Lily said, shrugging.

"If my parents send me something good that I can share, you three will get some," Sierra promised. Lily nodded a thanks to her as she looked back at the object that had gained all their interest. Gingerly reaching out, her fingers traced the metal, causing a wave of exhaustion to flow over her like water from a shower. Recoiling, Lily leaped off the bed and stared at the amulet.

"The amulet's making me tired."

"Interesting…" Sierra mused. "There must be something about you, Lily, that the amulet just doesn't like."

"Perhaps I should be the one to hold on to it then," Victoria said, wrapping the amulet in a bit of cloth and shoving the bundle into her pocket.

"C'mon. Scotty said that he'd be in the common room to study," Sierra said as she gathered her books up in her arms.

Lily sighed inwardly. It wasn't Scotty's fault that he was struggling with magic, and she wasn't blaming him for needing their help. He was trying really hard and putting in the effort to succeed. But Lily wasn't going to lie, tutoring him was stressful. Lily's hair had already been singed once, and Sierra had nearly been skewered twice by an errant quill that was being used as a practice subject.

"What's the focus today? Please tell me it isn't protections against the dark magical arts," Victoria begged.

"He muttered something vaguely about transfiguration and herbology."

"This should be painless," Amara said, already in motion toward the door.

Lily hoped that was the case today. If not, then she was using Amara as a human shield.

((☆))

DAYS PASSED, AND STILL they had failed to learn anything new about the amulet in their possession. The only thing they had learned was that Lily could touch and hold the amulet without any exhaustion consuming her, as long as it was wrapped up in cloth. Her skin just couldn't touch it. So, she was holding on to it instead of Victoria now. But its mystery plagued them all whenever they tried to decipher it, and they were trying hard.

Whenever they weren't working on their schoolwork, they were doing more research on the amulet and continuing their going-nowhere research on its ancient runes. Thanks to Amara, they knew the runes read of protection wards and a containment spell. Its purpose was still clear as mud though. Lily was on the verge of tearing her hair out in frustration at this.

"Lily!" Bella ordered, snapping her attention back onto her aunt. "Did you hear me?"

"Sorry. I was lost in thought," Lily confessed as she remembered she was spending a rare afternoon off with her aunt. And they were in her aunt's quarters no less! She shoved thoughts of the amulet to the back of her mind for the time being.

"What were you thinking?" Bella inquired. "You were really lost in whatever it was."

"Well…" Oh boy, Lily, think! She couldn't tell Bella the truth. Everything would go down the toilet. Maybe a half-truth. "Ancient runes.

Amara showed us some from a letter she received from her grandmother."

"If you have questions on anything to do with ancient magic, Sirius is who you should ask," Bella said, a wariness in her expression. "For my own curiosity, why is she showing you ancient runes?"

"Well, I may have asked her to teach me more about sirens, and she thought that showing her language was a good first step." Lily wasn't exactly lying about this. She had asked Amara, and the siren was showing Lily her native language, just not runes. Ocean dwellers didn't use runes. But Bella didn't necessarily need to know that part.

"Oh. How thoughtful," Bella said relaxing again with a small smile.

That was a close one. Lily was sure that she couldn't afford any more close calls like that. She focused on her aunt as Bella began telling a funny story from dinner the other night. Each teacher would covertly steal something off of Presnell's plate as he rambled on about a goblin rebellion until he noticed that his plate was empty and he hadn't eaten anything. Lily couldn't believe that she hadn't noticed that…

❨ ☆ ❩

Lily was awoken from her sleep that night by a strange glow that lit up their room. At first, with her sleep-addled brain, Lily thought it was Amara and her eyes until she realized it wasn't green. Confused and now wide awake, she looked around, finding the amulet on her nightstand glowing underneath the cloth. The glow was—oddly enough—a crimson glow. Lily sat up in bed amazed that it was dimly lighting the entire room. It was actually because of that Lily noticed Amara staring at the amulet too. Lily had no idea how the amulet could even glow— let alone red—or where the glow was coming from. Despite all the uncertainties, however, one thing was blatantly clear to Lily: this was all kinds of not good.

"I think we have a problem," Lily whispered.

"We must put it back," Amara urged.

Lily shook her head.

"No. It's still safer with us here."

"Then we should alert the professors."

"And get in trouble," Lily pointed out.

Amara frowned at her, clearly not caring. But then the glow vanished abruptly, plunging the room into darkness. This wasn't good at all.

"At least I was brought along under protest," Sierra whispered groggily.

"No matter what we do, one side or the other will come down on us," Victoria said sleepily with a yawn.

Great, now they were all awake. Stupid amulet.

"I'd prefer professors before a dark witch," Amara remarked.

"I'd prefer to continue this debate in the morning," Lily groaned. "It's only one in the morning, guys."

"This *will* be discussed," Amara hissed.

To say that the rest of that night wasn't the best sleep Lily ever had was an understatement. She doubted she slept longer than forty-five minutes at a time. So when the sun rose and peered through the windows, Lily was happy in a weird way. But she was also dreading it since their conversation was now going to happen. As soon as she opened her eyes, Amara's emerald ones were staring at her. She wondered if the siren had stared at her for the remainder of that night. She hoped this would be painless, but Lily was doubting it.

"We must return it," Amara said plainly. It was clear that she would not be swayed from her position.

"And risk it being taken?" Lily asked as she propped herself up in her bed.

"Nothing's been tried in a while, Lily. Maybe the danger to it and you has—" Sierra was cut off by a massive explosion.

The entire dorm building shook as they were all knocked out of their beds, their bodies smacking the hard stone floor, surely leaving bruises. Even some of the windows cracked from the blast. Screams of utter panic and fear filled the air from the other rooms as the shaking subsided. All four of them sat there staring at one another wide-eyed as the screams grew in number and then turned into frantic shouts. Lily grabbed the wrapped amulet, shoving it into her pocket. Then she wrapped her outer cloak around her before rushing into the common room, where everyone was quickly congregating.

Everyone was in various states of wakefulness and dress, most in their pajamas still, hair a mess, and looking like they were slapped awake. Then again, they all kind of were. Only three first years were in their school robes, and those were on haphazardly at best. Several more were half in them and half out. The only thing they all had in common this morning was their nervous chatter and petrified-with-fear looks. Scotty was dripping wet in his bathrobe, standing at their usual couch. Lily eyed him, making him scoff at her.

"I was in the shower."

"This early?" Victoria asked.

"Only way I can get warm water," Scotty grumbled. "What was that though?"

"We don't know, but whatever it was, it was…" Lily stopped talking, seeing Bella rushing down the stairs, her fluffy black skirts billowing out behind her with Sirius, Nikki, Professor Orion, and a couple Themidas behind her. They appeared stressed, and Professor Orion looked the most energetic and spry that Lily had ever seen the elderly principal all year—or in her life, come to think of it.

Then his voice bellowed out through the room. "*Lily Hale?*"

Conversation ceased as all eyes fell upon her. She shifted how she was standing, uncomfortable at the sudden attention on her.

"Yes?" she replied timidly.

Bella, Sirius, and Nikki rushed to her protectively as Orion visibly relaxed.

"Thank Merlin, you are safe." He turned to the Themidas. "No one leaves this building until the perimeter is secure. Begin your manhunt."

The Themidas nodded grimly and then rushed off as Professor Orion remained on the steps.

"All classes today are canceled! No one is permitted to roam outside of this level or building until your professors say otherwise. Breakfast will be delivered here to your common room. More of this situation will be explained later. For now try to relax and enjoy this day off."

Everyone looked a little more relieved that whatever situation was unfolding was being handled, but some were giving Lily curious glances. She looked between Bella, Sirius, and Nikki as they scanned the room, almost like they were waiting for an opponent to appear out of thin air. Lily gently laid her hand on Bella's right hand, which at present was gripping her wand so tightly that her knuckles were white. The moment their skin touched, Bella looked at her tensely. This was not how Bella normally was, and Lily was alarmed.

"What's going on?" Lily asked quietly.

"Nothing that you need to worry about right now," Bella replied, voice deeply concerned.

"I suggest that everyone go back to their rooms and get dressed," Nikki ordered.

Everyone nodded at the request, but no one moved.

"Once you return, breakfast will be presented!" Orion called.

Begrudgingly, they all slowly headed off to their dorms to throw on some clothes.

"On the bright side, at least you can finish your shower now, Scotty," Sierra teased, making Victoria giggle. He snorted at her with a scowl.

"No way! Getting thrown to the floor once in the shower is more than enough for today!"

"C'mon. Off to get dressed," Nikki prodded.

Lily and her group headed off in their separate directions to their sides of the dorms as Bella followed the girls closely. Nikki and Sirius drifted back to Orion's sides on the stairs, seemingly like sentries or watchdogs. Lily walked down the hallway of the girls' dorm being hyperaware of Bella's presence right against her back as they walked. Almost closer than her shadow. Entering their room, Lily finally turned and eyed her aunt as her friends filed in around them.

"Aunt Bella—"

"I'm staying by your side."

"For something that I don't need to worry about?" Lily replied, crossing her arms over her chest.

"Precisely. So you'd better get used to it. I'd have thought you'd be thrilled."

"Happy to spend time with you. Not to be watched like a hawk," Lily retorted.

"Too bad," Bella replied, unmoved.

Lily groaned out in frustration, grabbed her clothes, and headed for the bathroom. Thankfully, Bella remained out with Lily's friends to give her some privacy. Small miracles.

Upon completing her bathroom routine, Lily vacated it reluctantly for Sierra to replace her. Amara was lounging on her bed with a textbook as Victoria was nervously eyeing Bella, who was mending the cracked windows with magic. Lily's gut was telling her that the explosion was an attempt to steal the amulet. That was why Themidas were on a manhunt. That was why everyone was so concerned about her. That was why the school was now in lockdown. Bella looked at her, and after a few moments of an intense stare off, Bella dropped her arms and sat down upon Lily's bed.

"I'm not going to explain what's going on, Lily. So stop looking at me like you've been betrayed."

Lily had had enough. "Let me tell you what I know, and you will fill in the gaps, Aunt *Isabella*."

Bella winced at Lily using her full name and the way in which she had used it.

"I know the ogre incident is connected to what's going on right now. I know that the Themidas are present to secure the school because of breaches to school grounds all year. And I know Sinestra is involved because I forced it out of Professor Nero when she came to check up on my safety following Christmas. So what is it you aren't telling me? What's happened?"

Bella sighed and rubbed her eyes with her hands.

"Why couldn't you take after Callista right now instead of me?" Bella moaned. "Fine. Yes, Sinestra is involved. Some of her followers just blew a hole in the basement wall of the school to retrieve an artifact for their dark lady. We're now concerned that she'll focus on you to finish what she started eleven years ago."

"Did they get it? This artifact?" Of course Lily already knew the answer.

"It appears so. That's why you aren't allowed anywhere without a teacher," Bella stressed.

Lily relaxed her stance and softened her tone too. "You can tell me things, Aunt Bella. I'm not a child." She sat down beside her aunt who wrapped an arm around her shoulders.

"Yes, you are a child, Lily. But I'll…be more transparent with dangers that are directed at you. OK?"

"OK," Lily conceded. "You can trust me."

"I know I can, Lily," Bella whispered.

A clearing of a throat broke them out of their moment together.

"Hate to interrupt," Nikki said from the doorway, "but Orion wants to talk to you."

"Coming." Bella sighed.

It was clear this wasn't a pleasant conversation she was going to have with the principal. Hesitantly, Bella left the room, and Nikki replaced her.

"OK, who's next?" Sierra asked, exiting the bathroom. Victoria happily went next. Amara was last. Nikki watched as they all practiced their transfiguration tasks and skills, giving feedback to them along the way. Lily wasn't minding the bodyguard if they all got private lessons like this. Too bad Scotty wasn't there right then. He could really use the private lessons…

"THAT AMULET WAS WARNING us about what was going to happen," Lily said the moment Bella left them alone to go to sleep that night. She and Sirius would be camping out in the common room for the night on guard duty. It was most likely that way on all the other floors as well with the plethora of teachers. Student safety was their main focus.

"That must be the reason why Sinestra wants it. It'll warn her if danger is nearby so she can avoid it," Sierra hypothesized.

"I find myself agreeing," Amara admitted. "We were right to take it to deprive her of such a powerful object. Especially since her followers went to such lengths to destroy the wall and presumably the pool."

"But now we have to protect it," Victoria pointed out.

Thus, their issue.

Being that they were only first years, now in possession of some early-warning amulet that the most powerful dark witch of all time just tried to acquire, they were totally out of their means. Their knowledge of protections against the dark magical arts was minimal. They couldn't tell anyone without fear that they'd be severely punished for stealing it and breaking (probably) a bunch of school rules. Not to mention Lily was being watched constantly because the professors thought that she was in danger now from said dark witch. It seemed that their problems just kept compounding upon themselves.

"We'll form a plan with Scotty in the morning. Hopefully we'll get a few seconds alone," Lily decreed. "We're better when all of us are together."

"You mean we're more troublesome when all of us are together," Sierra muttered.

"Isn't that the same thing?" Lily asked with a smile, making them all laugh. It was enough to ease the tension that had been building up since that morning. "Good night, everyone."

"Good night, Lily," the others said in unison as they settled down in their own beds. Lily only hoped that she slept more this night than she had the previous night, because she'd need it in order to brainstorm a plan.

CHAPTER XII
THE GATEWAY

"Now, remember, the roots of the dognape have toxins on them, so don't touch them. Merely clip them with your scissors, and re-plant the main sapling. You'll learn in potions just how useful dognape roots are in various potions," Professor Poppy Samsona, the herbology teacher, instructed. She was a petite, round woman with graying short blond hair. Her unique yellow eyes appeared catlike with her friendly and bubbly demeanor.

Lily normally loved herbology since she was able to get all hands-on with the subject matter and help the plants out. She didn't want to toot her own horn, but she had a very green thumb…when she wanted to. But today, she just wanted class to be over with.

Four days had passed since the amulet was "stolen," and in her possession, not nearly as safe as she thought it was, and Lily had personal guards in every professor in every class. Even now, Samsona was standing over her shoulder as a guard while she taught the class. The only class they had that was somewhat normal was protections against the dark magical arts (or PADMA as the students had come to call the class), and that was only because Sirius and Bella were there so they didn't have to hover. She finished planting both parts of her dognape and pushed them forward on the table as a yelp came from Felix Cooper—Scotty's roommate—further down the table. He was rubbing his arm after it was pinched by a nearby wolfsnare plant.

"It looks like some sixth years didn't fully feed their wolfsnare this morning. Shame on them," Professor Samsona chastised.

Lily smirked and leaned back, checking to see if she'd planted her dognape crooked. Seeing it was planted perfectly and after Poppy checked her off with a satisfied smile, she gathered up her things and left with Scotty and Victoria.

"That's about the only class I don't need any help with," Scotty whined. And so it began yet again.

"That isn't true. You didn't need help in broom flying. You really don't need it in rune studies and care of magical creatures and beasts," Victoria argued for perhaps the hundredth time.

"Yet I suck at charms, transfiguration, protections against the dark magical arts, and potions!"

"To be fair, potions gets everyone from time to time, including Sierra," Lily mentioned. "Plus, you don't suck at protections. Aunt Bella applauded your recent demonstration, if you remember."

"Be that as it may, I still can't get things as easily as you guys. It's frustrating!" Scotty retorted.

"Maybe you're just trying too hard," Victoria advised. "You're forcing it to happen instead of letting it come naturally."

"Hmm…" Scotty thought about it for a long moment. "Maybe you're right, Vic."

"That is a good point," Lily added. Why hadn't she thought of that pearl of wisdom?

A short walk down the halls later and they were back in the comforts of the first-year common room. Amara and Sierra were already at their couch, having left herbology class earlier. Seriously, how did Sierra complete the lesson so fast? She normally had a harder time with herbology because—in her words—the plants hated her. Lily sat down with a plop between the bookworm and the siren upon the couch.

As was becoming usual these days, Bella arrived mere minutes after they did at the common room and stood unobtrusively in the corner. It was because of that constant presence that they hadn't been able to brainstorm a plan to keep the amulet safe. Lily was tempted to have them smuggle Scotty into their dorm room so they could just talk it over. It wasn't like they hadn't already broken rules this year.

"Lily, how is it that you're so gifted in magic anyway?" Scotty asked, still slightly glum.

Lily decided that humor was the perfect route to take with this.

"Simple. I'm a Black. We're the best," Lily said and smiled. Bella chuckled from the corner, making all of the kids turn to look at her.

"You really are more of a Black than you are a Hale." Bella said with a smirk.

"See? Any Black is just naturally amazing," Lily said, lifting her chin haughtily.

Everyone burst out laughing, Bella's cackles bouncing off the walls. Even Lily giggled at her own antics. That was the ticket. No more depressing thoughts were needed.

"On a serious note," Victoria still giggled, "can we go over the stuff from rune studies? I was a little confused about it."

"Sure." Lily giggled back. "Where do you want to start?"

❨ ☆ ❩

"Now, remember, the disarming spell is one of the most vital and useful spells that you could have at your disposal when facing down an opponent. For beginners like you, this spell could mean the difference between life and death in a fight. Not that I expect you to find yourself dueling some dark opponent anytime in the near future, you are first years, but one can never be too prepared," Bella instructed as she paced the length of the classroom, which had been cleared of desks so they could practice. By their offices, Sirius stood to assist Bella with a small demonstration.

"I know we've covered the wand movement and the pronunciation in the last few classes, so just watch closely as I use them to disarm Professor Ryker."

"*Try* to disarm, sweetheart," Sirius returned, making her roll her eyes with a smirk.

"Sorry, *try* to disarm, darling Sirius," Bella said, getting chuckles.

Lily loved their banter since it happened so flawlessly and naturally. It really was no wonder that they became best friends. They were like two halves of one whole, not complete unless they were together, side by side.

Plus, it just added an extra layer of fun in class whenever they teamed up for things…like right now.

"Bring it on, Bella!" He waved at her, wand firmly clasped in his right hand.

"*Exarmaueris!*" Bella called and sent the spell right at Sirius's torso. The blue spell sailed through the air at him very quickly, but before it would have hit him, he moved his wand in front of himself, wordlessly casting the shield spell they'd learned weeks ago and causing the blue orb to turn into white splatters as it struck it and dissipated.

"That is the only course of action you should take aside from diving for cover if you're being attacked by most spells. As we've covered numerous times, the shield spell *obstructionum* will be your best friend but not always will the offending spell dissipate like that. Most of the time, it will bounce off the shield in any direction, causing absolute chaos. Only with lots of experience, focus, and an advanced technique will that be the result," Bella instructed. She then proceeded to pair everyone off to practice on their own with both spells.

Lily got partnered with Sierra for a change instead of Amara, and they began their practice. Disarming was fairly simple, but catching the opposing wand out of the air was harder. On the flip side, the shield spell was still a major challenge to perfect. It took several attempts—and several disarmings—before Lily and Sierra had somewhat mastered their shield spells. Amara had mastered hers as well, along with Victoria, who seemed to have a natural talent for dueling spells and curses. Scotty, surprisingly, mastered both on his first try with Victoria, earning praise from both Bella and Sirius.

"I'm sure Ms. Holton appreciates your excellent performance," Sirius said, winking. Scotty blushed at the comment.

"I knew you could do it, Scotty," Victoria said and smiled.

"Thanks," Scotty replied and smiled back at her. Perhaps Scotty's struggles with magic were coming to an end now.

Lily felt equal parts relieved and happy at the same time. Of course, the shield spell would have come in handy prior to now with all of the unintended reactions from his various magical attempts. Maybe Lily should suggest teaching that earlier in the year to Aunt Bella. It could help out other first years.

《 ☆ 》

FINALLY, THE DAY EVERYONE was looking forward to had arrived. Today was when they all would get their packages from home. Throughout the morning, owls arrived from all over with various different things and goodies. Everything from the standard letters that always came to small packages and medium boxes was delivered to the dorms.

Lily marveled at the scene, how beautiful it was and how much it resembled an aerial dance. No owl collided with another in their movements. They always managed to avoid one another at the last moment. She wondered idly if the owls had practiced this flying mastery beforehand, but that was impossible since they had no idea where the intended recipient of the packages would be, come time.

Slowly the packages were delivered and opened by their recipients with friends hovering close, eager to see what was inside. Scotty was the first of their group to get his gift. It was a small package with a letter tied together. After quickly reading through his letter, he smiled and tore into the package as though it were Christmas morning. Lily found herself smiling along too as he revealed the object inside.

But her smile quickly faded at the sight of two halves of a once-decorative mirror that easily appeared to be from the Victorian era in age. A series of animals and magical creatures were all around the tarnished silver frame, the edge where it was broken had been rounded so it wouldn't cut anyone handling it. *That* was his gift? It seemed like something that should've been thrown away instead. It looked like junk.

"I don't get it," Victoria said, scowling. "Why're you so excited for just an old broken mirror?"

"It's not just some old broken mirror. It's way more than that. Here." Scotty handed one half to Victoria and held the other half in his hands, as though he were examining his own reflection. Lily scooted over beside Victoria and peered at the mirror in her hands, seeing Scotty's smiling face in it.

"What the—"

"It's a communication system. I guess it was a fad back in the 1820s. My mom had this when she was at Gerhardt to talk to her own grandmother. From what she told me, it sounds like my great-grandmother preferred this to letters since she had a hard time writing in her later years, and that was why she gave it to my mom. I'd asked my mom for it so I could talk to you guys more when we're in our dorm rooms."

"That's ingenious, Scotty!" Lily beamed. This would solve so many of their problems!

"Well, I know it was hard for us to really plan given the obvious limitation. Besides, I kind of talk more with you all than I do my own roommates, so not being able to talk at night is a little…depressing, sometimes."

"I'm putting this in our room," Victoria vowed, rushing off.

Scotty took his half and did the same, looking rather pleased with himself for the idea. Both of them returned to their couch just as another package landed gracefully in front of them. This time, it was for Sierra, who excitedly reached for it.

Inside were various things all grouped together. There were supplies for her braces, some delicious-looking soft pastries in plastic bags, and a brand-new book included as well (shocker). After Sierra divided up some of the pastries, with everyone moaning in delight from the flavor of said pastries, she carried her box with the remaining items to their room. With their excitement over, Lily looked around the common room, seeing just how ridiculous it was with all of the deliveries that were being dropped off. All the students were showing off their hauls to their friends and certain individuals that were shocked at what their families had sent to them.

"Duck!" Amara yelped just as Lily saw an owl with an obscenely large box diving right down at her.

Lily managed to hit the floor just as the owl and package collided into her spot on the couch. A couple of seconds later, the owl hopped up on top of the box, looked angrily at it and then at Lily, and hooted its opinion on the task it was given. Once it was finished sounding off, it flew off on its way, leaving the package on the couch where it had crashed.

"I think it said you can deliver it from here!" Sierra giggled.

"Well, given the size of this thing…poor bird," Lily sympathized. She moved the box from the couch onto the floor to reclaim her seat.

"Who does it belong to?" Scotty asked.

"Um…It says Lily," Amara remarked, reading the label.

Lily straightened in her seat.

"What? Let me see," Lily demanded.

Sure enough, it said, "Lily Hale," on the tag. The sender's name was also present too: Proxima Nero. Well, this was a happy surprise.

"Hmm…Aunt Proxima sent me something."

"As in Professor Nero's mom?" Victoria asked, shocked.

"Yeah. Maybe Professor Nero asked her to send something for me," Lily suggested. It would fit with Nikki's character. She'd have to send a thank-you off to her cousin's mom. After opening up the box and removing the packing materials, Lily and her friends gripped the sides of the box, huddling around it to see what was inside.

Positioned in the center was a beautiful trophy cup of gold. The engraved writing was hard to make out with it inside the box, and it looked like it had been damaged at some point in time. However, the engraved rune design around the lip of the cup was pristine, as though it had been completed yesterday. It was confusing. Her mother had zero trophies. Bella had confirmed that she wasn't athletic, so why would Lily get a trophy cup from Proxima?

"An odd gift to get," Scotty mused.

"I wonder why she gave it to me," Lily confessed.

"The answer might be on the engraving plate in front," Sierra pointed out.

"Be careful. It looks broken," Victoria advised.

Lily reached for it with her right hand, her left still holding onto the box that all her friends were at the same time Amara stiffened and wrinkled her nose.

"The gold smells funny."

"You can smell gold?"

"No. That's why it—"

"Lily! *Stop!*" Bella and Nikki yelled in unison, sprinting through the common room with Sirius just behind them.

Panic was clear on all three of their faces as they rushed through the chaotic room, dodging packages, owls, and other students. But it was too late.

Lily's fingers touched the rim of the cup as they spoke, and the entire common room blurred. The screams of her aunt and cousin vanished as the sense of apparition washed over her, except it wasn't a normal apparition. It felt like the floor had just given out underneath them. Her entire body felt like it was ripped apart cell by cell. After enduring this level of agony for several long seconds, Lily's brain kicked itself back into functioning, and she let go of the cup.

It was the most unpleasant sensation that Lily had ever had. But the moment Lily let go, she felt herself get yanked back to the ground, her body impacting the rocky ground hard, knocking the wind from her.

For a couple seconds, Lily just lay there, allowing her stomach to settle and air to return to her aching lungs. Once those things happened, she pushed herself up from the rocky ground and looked around. The familiar setting of the common room was gone, and replacing it appeared to be a slightly smooth rocky ground that her friends had been deposited on. The lighting was dim compared to what they had come from in the dorm room, but it was still enough for Lily to make out her friends. Amara was an arm's length away, kneeling at the ready for a threat and examining the area around them looking fine. Sierra and Scotty were both groaning a few feet away and getting up themselves, several minor scrapes on their hands. Even further away, in a sort of rut in the stone, was Victoria lying with the now-empty box. Her eyes were closed, blood running from her hairline down the left side of her face, and her right leg was twisted at an unnatural angle, clearly broken. Crawling over to the other redhead in alarm, Lily shook her shoulder slightly.

"Vic? Vic!" Lily cried frantically.

"Vic, wake up!" Scotty added now beside her.

Sierra pressed her fingers to Victoria's neck and then sighed in relief.

"She's alive, guys. Calm down. Her pulse is good and strong. She's just unconscious."

"Which is likely for the best," Amara opined gesturing to Victoria's broken leg. Lily found herself agreeing. Seeing her leg at that angle was beginning to make Lily's stomach churn uncomfortably. She turned her attention to the item that was responsible for this so she didn't puke.

"Where's the cup?"

"Over there," Scotty said. He crawled over to it and examined it closely. "Huh."

"What?" Sierra asked, beating Lily to the punch.

"It's dated from 1703, England. I can't make out for what though."

"That's great, Scotty, but not helpful right now," Lily moaned.

Scotty looked at her and pursed his lips. "How about the fact that this is an illegal gateway?"

"What's a gateway?" all three girls asked in unison.

"I'm not surprised you guys don't know about them. My mom showed me one because they're so hard to make. That's the only reason I know. They're ridiculously rare and highly regulated. The creation of an illegal gateway can get you sent to Xurban for life. It's right up there with the forbidden curses in terms of severity."

"You still haven't answered what it is," Sierra complained.

"A permanent apparition line. There are only five legal gateways in the world. They're used in places where there's a lot of travel and long distances. The main one I know of is from the Magical Congress in Philadelphia to the British Parliament of Magic in London. I guess they were misused a lot in the early 1700s."

"OK, so it brought us from Gerhardt to a dark, damp, rocky cave," Lily whined. This was great, absolutely great.

"Actually, based on the number of stalagmites and stalactites, this is a cavern," Sierra corrected—as if that really mattered at the moment.

Cave, cavern, same difference as far as Lily was concerned. They were away from where they should be.

"More than a cavern."

Amara's tone made all three of them spin around and face the direction the siren was staring in. Lily instantly gave a lot more credit to whoever really sent that cup to her. They hadn't just sent Lily and her friends to some random cavern somewhere. No, they'd planned to send them there, to *this* place. The only thing Lily's gut was telling her was that this was a trap.

And Lily just fell right for it.

CHAPTER XIII
RUINS

Directly in front of them, on a peninsula of sorts, were the ruins of a once glorious city. The area was illuminated by natural daylight, but that was impossible since there was no opening to allow it in. It could only be there through magical means. The architecture could've easily belonged to the ruins in ancient Greece or Rome. It was probably related in some way. Around the peninsula were steep cliffs with waterfalls crashing down on the other side of the cavern, beyond the city from cutouts in the cavern wall. Lily had no idea how far down the drop was, but she didn't want to find out.

But the ruined city was drawing her eye again. Clearly in its prime, this was a highly prized place to be. Maybe this was like the capital of a series of cities. Now, however, most of the buildings were destroyed or severely damaged. At the entrance to the city was an elaborately constructed and massive arch with runes engraved upon it. There weren't any words to describe the majesty of this place.

"I don't believe it." Sierra gasped in awe.

"Is this really…" Scotty asked.

"I—I think so."

"OK…not to sound dumb, but what is it?" Lily asked.

Scotty and Sierra whipped their heads to look at her as though she had just gone insane.

"You're a Pureblood, Lily. Are you seriously saying you don't know what this place is?" Scotty asked, dumbfounded.

"No," Lily said, shrugging.

"This…" Sierra gestured to the ruins in front of them. "…is one of the Seven Sanctuary Cities."

"You mean, wizards and witches built this to protect themselves?" Lily asked.

"Yes. Legend says that during all of the ancient hunts and purges, wizarding kind constructed seven hidden and highly protected cities for them to reside in without fear. It saved tons of lives. But when more and more Nonbloods threatened to expose the cities to the entire nonmagical world when they were denied more say in their democratic assemblies, tensions rose. Soon it boiled over into riots…then all-out civil war. The Purebloods and Halfbloods began to wonder why they were even bothering to hide when they were massacring the Nonbloods with relative ease in combat. That's how the blood purity ideal began.

"Eventually all of the cities were ruined battle zones and sickly ghettos, leading to them being completely abandoned. As time passed, the locations were lost and the cities just became legend. In 1618, two were found out of the seven, changing that. This is now number three," Sierra finished.

"So we've been transported to a highly significant historical site," Lily summarized.

Sierra and Scotty glanced at one another.

"Yeah," Scotty admitted with a shrug. "In plain terms."

Well, there were worse places to be, that was for sure. However, considering they were sent there, this was probably a very bad place to actually be, especially alone…and particularly since it looked deserted. There was something big going on there. But what was the endgame?

"Well, let's get that cup and go back." Lily had no sooner finished speaking than a loud "pop" sounded, causing everyone to look and see the cup now gone.

"Do we have a working plan B?" Amara asked drily.

"Nope." Lily scowled. They were now officially trapped. "C'mon, guys. We need to see what we've got to work with here."

"No, Lily, we need to stay with Victoria," Sierra said fearfully.

"OK, but we have no idea when help will arrive, and eventually Vic is going to wake up. So you want us to remain right here, exposed and without shelter from who knows what is here? Let's face it, guys: we need some sort of shelter if we're here overnight. We need to plan and prepare for anything here," Lily countered.

Everyone looked at one another.

"Lily's got a point," Scotty reluctantly admitted.

"I will stay with Victoria," Amara volunteered. "Those runes prevent me from entering the city anyway. I'm of more use to Victoria right now."

"All right. I promise we won't be long, Amara," Lily vowed.

Amara nodded back to her, eyeing Lily with worry. Lily had the sinking feeling they all needed to worry.

Together, Lily, Sierra, and Scotty headed off for the ruined city… and whatever was awaiting them inside.

(☆)

As far as shelter went, the buildings were a crapshoot. Aside from the fact that Amara wouldn't be able to use any of them, the ones that appeared to be in OK shape structurally were beyond filthy on the inside, as animals had made their own homes there. This forced them to press deeper into the city in search of better conditions, which didn't seem to exist. The ruins did look like they'd been through a war of unseen proportions, however. Some of the buildings looked like they were barely standing. Yet, despite this, Lily was enjoying walking through this city. The history was captivating to her…especially when she knew that there wasn't going to be a sudden lecture about a goblin uprising at any moment.

"I've got a bad feeling about this," Sierra complained.

"Yeah, we've seen how it is here; there's nothing. We should head back," Scotty added.

Lily wanted to argue and keep exploring, but she knew it was smarter to go back. They'd been gone from Amara and Victoria long enough as it was.

"OK. Let's go," Lily conceded. She really didn't want to fight her friends any more than she already had, especially under these conditions. They needed to be unified.

They'd just turned around when a loud explosion sounded above them on a high crumbling building with lots of plant growth upon it. On instinct, Scotty shoved Lily and Sierra backward just as stone and vegetation rained down at them. Lily curled up into the fetal position and waited as the avalanche of debris rained down on them and the street.

Once the sound of debris falling had quieted down, Lily uncurled herself and blinked rapidly. Coughing, she got to her knees and saw

Sierra sitting up and coughing as well, unharmed minus inhaling a lungful of dust. But Scotty…

"Scotty!" Lily yelled in a panic. She and Sierra started to climb up the steep giant pile of rubble but ended up sliding back down just as fast.

"Scotty!" Sierra cried equally in a panic.

For all they knew, he was completely buried and slowly suffocating. None of this would have happened had Lily not touched that damned cup. "Scotty, where are you?"

"Guys?" his voice called, and then he coughed several times. "Are you OK?"

"Yes! Are you?" Lily demanded. Relief flooded her that he wasn't dead.

"I think so. My legs are pinned though, so I'm not going anywhere."

"We're on it!" Lily called. She and Sierra began to levitate the pieces before Scotty's agonizing scream from the shifting rubble stopped them.

"Stop! The debris is highly unstable on my side. You're going to have to find a way around!" Scotty yelled.

"We're going to hurry! Don't worry!" Sierra called.

They rushed off together.

The plan was simple: keep going deeper into the city until there was a side street they could use to circle back and free Scotty from his impromptu tomb. But as they ran, they could find no side streets. They stopped to catch their breath for a moment at what appeared to be the far end of the city where the more prominent wizards clearly lived if the larger buildings were any indication; a massive—and mostly intact—temple for government directly in front of them. Lily presumed this was once the assembly building. From what looked like the second and third stories, stone bridges peeled off to roofs over nearby buildings, which they could then scale down.

"You see it, Sierra?" Lily panted.

"Yeah," she returned. "But I don't like it."

"Do you have a better idea?" Lily asked.

Seeing that Lily had her, Sierra shook her head with a grimace. They only had one course of action now, and Lily was convinced it was planned that way. Pulling out their wands again, they advanced cautiously to the doorway.

Where Sierra bounced back and collapsed as if she had run into a glass door.

"Are you OK?" Lily asked, concerned, rushing back to her side.

Sierra rubbed her forehead, grimacing.

"Uh-huh," Sierra groaned. "What happened?"

"If I had to guess, there must be Nonblood wards in place so only Pureblood and Halfbloods can enter. Most likely left over from the war here."

"Let's just go back to Scotty. We…we can figure out a different way."

"Yeah. OK, Sierra, let's…go." Lily's eyes widened seeing what was now approaching the two young witches from all directions.

They looked like people but weren't. They were figures of varying heights and sizes, composed entirely of black sand. Doing a quick count, Lily discovered they were facing at least a dozen of these things, and they were all closing in on them fast in a weird jerking surge forward. There were no details about them, not even eyes. It was like they were empty shells of something that were doing the bidding of someone else. But she could feel their malicious intent just fine. Sierra gasped and sprang to her feet. Both girls backed up to the doorway.

They were trapped, as was the plan. Lily was regretting a lot of life decisions at this moment.

"Why—why did they stop?" Sierra asked.

Lily frowned in confusion at the scene. Why did they just suddenly stop? They now appeared to be guarding the entrance, about fifteen feet away. Lily looked between where she was standing and where Sierra was standing, noticing the key detail.

"I'm standing over the threshold," Lily remarked.

Sierra looked at her, standing just in front of it—where she'd hit the invisible barrier.

"So…they want you inside," Sierra reasoned.

"It looks like it."

"Lily." Sierra locked their gazes. "You know this is a trap, right? That whoever sent that cup is probably inside and is going to kill you."

"I know," Lily said through a tight throat. That was exactly what she didn't want to admit. It made it more real. Ignorance really was bliss.

"But you're going to go inside anyway," Sierra lamented.

"I can't let you guys get hurt any more than you already have for me. I need to try to keep you safe," Lily stressed.

Sierra looked like she wanted to argue the point or maybe start crying, but after glancing at the sandy figures again, she decided to just concede the point.

"Be safe."

"You too. Watch your back, Sierra," Lily advised. Sierra nodded, leveling her wand at the figures as Lily backed into the building more before turning around. Here goes nothing.

(☆)

LILY KEPT HER WAND drawn as she took in the place she now found herself. Its power of magic was palpable, almost infused into the surroundings. The room was easily three stories tall with lots of windows dotting the walls, showing the magnificent waterfalls beyond. Yet, despite the visual, you could hardly hear the water rushing down at all inside the building. Perhaps a silencing charm was in place. Some of the elaborate decor was still present in this building as well, unlike the others, which were stripped clean. Gold and silver—even some bronze—were still visible on pillars, creating various designs and runes. She had no idea what they said, but at this point, it was academic. She doubted that she'd live long enough to research it.

Ringed balconies were at the second- and third-floor levels, allowing a view down onto the main floor, where Lily now found herself. In its prime, it had to have been amazing to be in here if the pillars spoke at all to the elegance this place once possessed. Some sections, however, looked like they'd been blasted to pieces. An indicator that this had also hosted a battle of its own. That civil war had to have been vicious for all the damages it had inflicted.

Cautiously, Lily stepped into the direct center and peered around for the stairs to climb up. That would be the ideal outcome of this mess. But Lily knew better than to believe that was how things would go. These were less-than-ideal conditions. A crunch of stone underfoot on the far side of the room had her spinning and pointing her wand faster than she ever thought she could. But nothing was visible to her. She certainly hadn't imagined hearing a crunch of stone on a boot. Not that loud, at least.

"Show yourself! I know you're here!" Lily demanded.

"Your instincts serve you well, Lillian." A feminine voice spoke up.

The hairs on the back of Lily's neck stood up at hearing her full first name. No one called her that—not even Bella when she was mad. Maybe she would if Lily really pushed her, but she never did.

Emerging from a darkened corner filled with debris was a woman. She was wearing a form-fitted black dress, but at her waist, it flared out to brush the ground. A black cape flowed from her shoulders to the ground behind her with a hood built in that covered her head. An upside-down triangle at her chest showed off her cleavage as a segment of the black fabric curled around her neck and upper chest. Lily noticed that as the woman brought her arms out from behind her back the sleeves ended halfway down her hand and were nearly skintight. But none of that gained her attention as much as her face. Or what was covering it.

On her face was a silver mask that was glistening and shiny. It looked like the face of a skull with black sockets where the eyes should have been. It also had black engraved…something, where hair would've been from what was visible from underneath her black hood. Lily gripped her wand harder at seeing the woman clearly in the light. She really wished that the woman had stayed hidden now.

"I've waited so long to see you again. My, how you've grown," the woman purred in her altered voice. There were metallic overtones and a sinister doubling effect to it that just sent chills down your spine.

"Stay right there," Lily ordered.

"Afraid I'll bite?" the woman taunted.

"Well, there's a reason why you want me alone, so I'm not letting you get any closer. I'm not taking chances," Lily stressed.

The woman chuckled. "Smart, just like your mother and Aunt Isabella. You really do share more with her than you do your own mother."

"Don't talk about her!" Lily snarled.

The woman laughed now. "Struck a nerve?"

Lily glanced around, making sure that they were alone still. It would be her luck that there was an army here in the shadows for this. Maybe more of those black sandy things. The woman snorted, drawing Lily's attention back to her.

"No one will interrupt us, so don't worry."

"That's not very reassuring." Lily spat.

"No, it's *very* reassuring." The woman moved to the side, and Lily mirrored her. "A private conversation is so rare these days, don't you agree?"

Lily decided that since she was trapped at the moment, she might as well get some answers…and buy time for their rescue. She had a good idea who this was, but she wanted to be sure before she allowed herself to full-on panic. Besides, just because Lily didn't see a wand didn't mean that she wasn't armed.

"OK…why choose here to chat?"

"It's safe for us."

Lily hardly thought it was safe—particularly for her. "But why send the cup? Why not visit me yourself at Gerhardt? I have a nice room," Lily retorted to the woman's hearty laugh.

"I'm aware."

"Then why not? Are you scared?" Lily taunted now.

"Hardly." The woman's purr was full of malice. "But this place fits our conversation better. The cup was just a convenient mode of transport."

"And what, pray tell, will we be discussing?"

"You giving me that amulet you so helpfully stole for me," the woman said, her hand outstretched.

That was all Lily needed to hear. Her worst fear had just been confirmed. Here in this ruined city she had indeed walked right into a trap. The woman in front of her was Sinestra.

CHAPTER XIV

SINESTRA

"I don't know what you're talking about," Lily lied instantly.

On the outside, she was trying to portray fearlessness. On the inside, she was heavily panicking. Her parents' murderer was standing in front of her. Sinestra had wanted her to steal the amulet. She had somehow disabled the wards so Amara and she would find the hidden hallway. Then that explosion was to fool everyone into letting their guard down to indeed send that cup. She faked it being sent by Proxima so Lily wouldn't grow suspicious. So many pieces clicked together now. The saying that hindsight is twenty/twenty sure was accurate.

"I find it hard to believe. However, given your mother and aunt, I shouldn't be too surprised at you trying to lie your way out of danger." Sinestra sighed.

"Aha! So you admit I'm in danger!"

"Not from me," Sinestra said.

Lily believed that as much as she did that the sky was any color other than blue. Or that Sierra hated reading. Or that Amara hated water.

Or…well, you get the idea. She highly doubted anything that Sinestra said.

"Then who? We're the only two people here."

"Exactly. I'm afraid you're in danger from yourself. I want to help you."

"My parents' murderer wants to help me? Forgive me if I now call you a liar," Lily snarled.

Sinestra took a step forward now that they'd reached their starting spots again. Lily jerked her wand higher, ready to hex—or try to hex— this woman, this dark witch.

"Give me the amulet."

"I don't have it."

"It's inside your pocket. I know that siren out there helped you re- trieve it, and you've been hiding it from everyone. Now, give it to me," Sinestra demanded.

How she knew so many details boggled Lily's mind, since there was no way that there was a spy at the school—or she was highly confident that there wasn't a spy at the school.

The weight of the amulet in her pocket seemed heavier now. Lily reluctantly pulled the cloth-wrapped amulet out of her pocket and pointed her wand at it. She still had some control over this situation, and she was going to use it.

"Come any closer, and I'll destroy it."

All that did was make Sinestra bellow out in laughter. "How nice! Go ahead," she said before her voice hardened. "I dare you."

"Then you won't get it," Lily said, confused. This completely threw her for a loop.

"I know. I want that thing to be destroyed."

This was absolutely ridiculous. Why would Sinestra go through all the effort to steal the stupid thing if she only wanted to destroy it? Wasn't it useful as a warning system to the dark witch? Come to think of it, it never lit up the whole time they were there, nor before she touched the cup. So…was it not a warning system? If not, then what was so special about the amulet? Lily's thoughts must've been reflected on her face since Sinestra straightened.

"They never told you," she mused, a hint of surprise evident, "what all exactly happened that night twelve years ago, did they?"

"You killed my parents for no reason," Lily spat. "Senseless murder."

"I confess I did," Sinestra said simply. "But that wasn't my intent when going that night. Had your mother stayed away in your room and never tried to take me out from behind, then she'd be alive today. I swear it."

"So it's her own fault she's dead?" Lily fumed. What kind of reason was that?

Sinestra inhaled deeply before she spoke again. "Have you never questioned how it was that you alone survived that night from that house? How a killing curse sent errantly at your crib during the duel with your mother and me completely rebounded to the ceiling, and you were left untouched? As though there was a shield around you that made you untouchable? Something that should be impossible with the Forbidden Curses?"

No, she hadn't. She'd just assumed that she was nothing more than a witness. She was actually attacked? Sinestra had tried to kill her too? Even if it was sent errantly in the duel, it was directed at her! Why hadn't Bella told her that part? The dark witch sighed at that moment and shook her masked head.

"I never wanted to harm you of all people. But blind rage is hard to break out of. Particularly when Callista led me to your doorway, then into your room."

"How?" Lily choked out. "How was I all right?"

"How else? Your mother was far more prepared than that useless father of yours. She had Sirius Ryker use his vast knowledge. He used ancient magical wards on you and your crib. Anything to keep you safe. It was so clear afterward that I wanted to kick myself. I should've foreseen you being untouchable. But like I said, I didn't go there that night to kill *you*."

"How does that—"

"When the killing curse struck the wards, the trap was sprung on me. I was stripped of my powers." Sinestra cut her off. "That amulet in your hand holds them. Protected from me by even more protective wards. Or it was. It isn't anymore. The wards have been lifted."

"What?" Lily demanded. "No, they're still there."

"When you touched it, I'm willing to bet that something happened to you. Something that seemed strange to you. Am I correct?"

The wave of exhaustion came back to the forefront of her mind. Was that…was it some sort of reversal of the wards? Using her own energy to nullify those protections? But if that was the case, then why didn't it do the same to Victoria? She was a Pureblood too and held it in her bare hand longer than Lily had. Was it because she'd been the one to touch it first?

"You see? I need that amulet."

"To instill even more fear, pain, and loss!" Lily yelled, forcing her analysis of the amulet from the forefront of her mind. She needed to keep the conversation going.

"To become whole again," Sinestra countered. There was a hint of anger in her voice. "Living without your magic is like being confined in a too-small cell, constantly shackled and not allowed to sleep. It's a strain on you that you could never imagine. I want to be normal again!"

"Maybe this is a fitting punishment for all you've done. Ever think about that?"

This was dangerous to do. She was completely stalling for time at this point. Her only priority was to keep the amulet away from Sinestra, but she couldn't hand it off to Sierra. Even if she could, those sand guardian things wouldn't let Sierra pass by them to escape. Then there was Lily even leaving this building. Even without magic, she was sure Sinestra was more than resourceful enough to stop her. Maybe there were more of those sand guardian things in this room, hiding in the shadows after all, just waiting for a signal. She'd never reach the door.

"More like cruel and inhumane," Sinestra growled. "I'd rather be locked away in the worst cell in Xurban prison before living one more day in this *pathetic* state!"

"Like I've already said, a fitting punishment."

Sinestra clenched her fists as an inhuman snarl ripped itself from her throat thanks to her mask altering her voice. Yes, what she was doing was like poking an angry bear with a stick, and yes, this wasn't smart to do, but Lily had the amulet. Sinestra couldn't summon it to her. Her odds of saving her friends right then looked pretty good, even if her own survival was questionable. Saving her friends took priority.

"All right, Lillian," Sinestra angrily breathed out. She was trying to calm herself. "Since you insist on playing hard to get, allow me to tell you how this entire interaction will unfold."

"If you insist," Lily said, cocking her head to the side in an imitation of Bella.

"You'll unwisely test my patience, forcing my lovely guards outside to attack that Nonblood. If your resolve still remains after she's dead, then I'll send them after the Halfblood trapped beneath the rubble caused by several of my loyal Venatores Mortem. I doubt that you'd still have your resolve after that, but if you somehow do, then that siren and Pureblood will face my followers, who have no qualms about murdering children. This is the hard way…or you can choose the easy way and just *hand it over*."

Sinestra held her hand out for it demandingly. Lily hesitated. She'd officially poked the bear too much. This was a very real and serious threat. Lily didn't doubt for a moment that her friends would be attacked and killed if she refused to hand the amulet over. Sinestra's history guaranteed that any threat of violence she made was actually a promise. Lily was now backed into a corner, metaphorically speaking.

"How am I sure my friends will be OK if I hand it over?" Lily asked nervously.

"I have no intentions of harming anyone here. Give me the amulet, and we all leave here in peace," Sinestra vowed.

"We can't leave here, and I'm not trusting you at all to bring us home. So most likely I give this to you, and we're either abandoned here or killed anyway," Lily deduced.

"You won't be left alone here for long. Now hand it over."

"Not without assurances," Lily said, backing up a step. She doubted that assurances would be made or that promises would be kept if Sinestra actually agreed to any. Instantly, a wand slid into Sinestra's right hand from her sleeve somehow. This wand was the most unique wand Lily had ever seen.

A skull and crossbones was at the base of the wand in her palm, and there was a black grip where her hand was holding the wand. The rest of the wand—including the skull and crossbones—was a pure white. Lily had no idea what the wand was made out of, but it didn't look at all like bone. She also thought there was a thin silver band at the front of the black grip too but couldn't be sure now.

"Lily," Sinestra growled.

Lily shivered at the tone and at hearing her shortened name from the dark witch. It was so odd after the dark witch had used her full name exclusively up until then.

"Give me that amulet before you force my hand. I won't ask for it again."

"It still has its wards." Desperate, yes, but Lily tried anyway. "You can't touch it."

"No, it doesn't. Not since you touched it. Hand. It. *Over.*"

"I can't. *Exarmauris!*" Lily sent the spell at the dark witch in desperation.

Sinestra said she didn't have magic, but she lazily waved her wand, deflecting Lily's spell away harmlessly. As it happened, Lily's attention was momentarily drawn to the amulet. It suddenly felt ten times heavier and hotter in her hand. Then it hit Lily what was going on.

Sinestra was close enough that some of her powers were leaching out of the amulet without the wards being present to trap them inside completely.

Lily knew the dark witch before her was dangerous, but this showed just how dangerous. Lily backed up even more as Sinestra chuckled and shook her head. She was finding this amusing?

"Oh, Lily. You have a lot to learn," Sinestra cooed.

"*Exarmauris!*" Lily called again, only to be met by the same result.

"This is pointless, Lily. You're only delaying the inevitable."

"You can't get it!"

"I already have. Now stop being difficult!" Sinestra admonished.

Sinestra blocked two more spells from Lily before she sent a spell at the first year, blowing Lily to the side…and closer to her. It took Lily's brain a couple seconds to register what had just happened.

The dark witch had ricocheted the spell to hit her from a different angle than it would have in a normal dueling position. She knew from Bella that to ricochet a spell was a highly advanced skill that not just any wizard or witch could do. Getting to her knees, Lily sent another spell at the older woman to maintain some of the remaining distance. It was blocked like all the others were, with as little effort as one would use to swat away a mosquito.

"Has Isabella taught you anything? I'd expect more from her."

"I'm a first year!" Lily said defensively. Sinestra talking down about Bella struck a deep nerve with Lily.

"Be that as it may, you live with her. I would've taught you a lot more by this age. Made sure you were the superior dueler in any situation. Be it against a peer or an older, more experienced enemy. I guess Isabella is slipping in her skills. How unfortunate, really. Next to Sirius, she used to be the best."

Lily growled at the older woman, her Black temper igniting. "Ex—"

"Silence!" Sinestra ordered, striking Lily square in the chest when she twisted to fire her spell at the dark witch. The stunning spell momentarily turned her into a limp ragdoll sending her into a chunk of debris. "*Exarmauris.*"

The amulet flew from Lily's hand in a wide arc into Sinestra's waiting hand triumphantly. Lily's body felt now like she'd just gotten knocked off of a broomstick and slammed into the ground, like Sierra had when they were learning how to ride one at the beginning of the year and ended up lying on the ground more times than they were sitting on her broom. At the time, it was extremely funny, until Sierra confessed that she hated flying in general, and she was afraid of heights.

The air also had been knocked out of Lily as well—either from the spell or hitting the chunk of debris, she wasn't sure. Because of this, she could only watch helplessly and pant as Sinestra stared at the amulet in her hands.

"At long last!" she crowed. A flash of white from the tip of Sinestra's wand impacted the amulet, creating an ear-splitting metal shriek. Then the amulet shattered like glass in her hand. Instantly Lily saw—and felt—Sinestra straighten and grow more powerful.

"Mmm," Sinestra hummed. "Finally, I'm back to normal again. How I've missed this."

Lily struggled to her feet and stared down the dark witch. She was confident that Sinestra would no longer hesitate to kill her and her friends now that she'd gotten what she wanted. Worst yet, this was all her fault. Had she listened to her friends and not gone after that amulet, then none of them would be here now. Lily inched toward the door to bolt to Sierra, but unfortunately, it was her movement that gained Sinestra's attention again. She now looked healthier than she was mere moments before. This version of Sinestra was nothing like the version Lily had first met.

"Thank you for this, Lily. This wouldn't have been possible without you."

"I didn't do anything for *you*," Lily spat.

"True, you had no idea. But the statement is still true."

"I don't want to hear that! You manipulated me! You orchestrated everything!"

"Whatever lets you sleep at night," Sinestra said, waving a hand dismissively.

Lily bristled but looked again at the door. Fighting Sinestra had already proven to be foolish, so that left only one option open to her. Executing the better part of valor, Lily sprinted for the doorway and her escape, throwing an *exarmauris* over her shoulder blindly. Just a few more feet and—

Lily was yanked backward right to the center of the room, dragged on her stomach. Looking over her shoulder, she nearly screamed at seeing Sinestra directly over her at her side. She was far closer now than Lily ever wanted her to be. After flipping over onto her back, she scuttled away with her heart pounding in her rib cage. This was arguably scarier than facing down that ogre had been.

"Trying to leave so soon?" Sinestra taunted. "I'd think you'd want to get information out of me before you try to flee. Now's your chance."

"S-such as?" Lily asked, her voice wavering.

"Perhaps why you needed to touch the amulet for the wards to vanish?" Sinestra paused. "Seriously, I'm not doing anything threatening to you right now, so stop cowering, Lily."

She wasn't about to stop cowering. Sinestra could turn very threatening very fast. Lily wasn't stupid, and trusting Sinestra was as smart as jumping willingly into a bonfire for fun. Not smart at all.

"Lost your tongue?" Sinestra asked.

Lily shrank into herself in response.

"*Do* you know why?"

Lily shook her head. Since her track record right now of predicting events and understanding things correctly wasn't good, she decided to just let Sinestra talk. If the dark witch was talking, then she wasn't hurting her friends. Sinestra knelt about six feet away from Lily in a posture that looked nonthreatening, but it could just be a trick.

"Those wards require blood relation to undo them. Quite ingenious of Ryker, really. A nice failsafe. Any Pureblood wizard or witch would be able to hold it, but the wards would have been in place still, and just as strong as the day they were initially put up. I wouldn't have been able to touch it—"

"We aren't related," Lily managed.

"Oh, we're more alike than perhaps you know."

"We're nothing alike!" Lily snarled. It seemed anger temporarily overrode her fear. She wasn't about to be compared to this woman. This *monster*.

Sinestra chuckled.

"Oh, they never told you? Hmm…they must not trust you."

"Aunt Bella trusts me completely!" Lily snarled again.

"She does? Then why didn't she tell you about the amulet?"

"I…"

"See? Doesn't exactly sound like trust to me."

"She has her reasons," Lily fought back. But Sinestra did have a point, as begrudgingly as Lily had to admit it.

"Mmm, she does."

Sinestra straightened and glanced at the doorway. Lily followed her gaze but saw nothing. Then the sounds of spells being fired off in the distance filtered in to them. Lily's first thought was that Sierra was defending herself from the sand figures outside. So, the betrayal came at last. Lily felt slightly better knowing that the agonizing wait was over.

"It sounds like our time together is growing short. There's a lot for us to discuss still, too. We'll have to just cover the most important things then."

"No, we won't."

"Now, now, Lily, don't start being difficult again," Sinestra warned.

"They'll be here soon," Lily said, steeling herself. "You won't be leaving when they get here. If you're smart, you'll just let me go now."

"Still a lot to learn, Lily," Sinestra said, shaking her head. "But I'll escape. After all, Isabella will ensure you're safe and not focus on capturing me. Even though you're perfectly safe with me."

Lily's face must have shown her clear doubt.

"You *are* safe with me. I told you I'd never planned on killing you that night. Blame your father for that one. He was the only one in that mansion who deserved death."

"My father did not!" Lily fumed.

"Yes, he did! He was a *swine*! The lowest of lowly scum!" Sinestra bellowed. "You clearly have no idea who your father even was."

"I know he didn't deserve murder."

"Have they really told you nothing?" Sinestra demanded. "Or is it because of me?"

Lily stared back at the dark witch in anger. After a few seconds, Sinestra's body relaxed from her angry stance. Lily felt an understanding of something wash over the dark witch, like she had just put several missing pieces together.

"They really didn't tell you?" Sinestra sounded genuinely hurt. Her ego was her weakness? Interesting.

"Tell me what?" Lily demanded through her clenched teeth.

Sinestra lowered her hood, allowing Lily to see the black engraving was actually vines that simulated hair on her mask. Then the wand in Sinestra's hand moved across her face, the silver mask evaporating into black mist as it vanished. Now revealed was an absolutely normal-looking woman underneath. She was beautiful, no doubt about that, but she looked exhausted and gaunt. Probably fixable with time and rest, but it didn't do her any favors. Lily debated if she was from an ancient Pureblood family.

She had pure light-gray almost snowy-white hair—clearly natural—that was curled slightly and fell to approximately her midback. With the dress and cape, it was hard to tell exactly how long it was. It was definitely a unique attribute about her. There was a dusting of freckles across her cheeks and nose too that was kind of cute. Lily's eyes, however, were drawn to Sinestra's strikingly blue eyes. They were so blue that…wait a minute. They looked like liquid lakes. She had seen these eyes before, quite frequently. Lily was transfixed, staring into the dark witch's eyes. She was startled out of her stare when she spoke again, the altered voice gone, leaving in its place a melodic one.

"My real name, Lily, is Arianna Hale…your aunt."

CHAPTER XV
FLASHPOINT

Lily's brain officially shut down. There was no way that the most evil and powerful dark witch in history was Lily's aunt. They couldn't be related. They just couldn't be. If this was true, then Bella would have told her. She would have prepared her for this remotely possible moment. Bella trusted her; she had said it herself. But those eyes…they were Lily's. She thought back to the photo of her mother and thought she had blue eyes. Yeah, that had to be it. Callista had blue eyes, so she got them from her.

"Lily," Sinestra's voice made Lily gasp again. It was so much of a shock, the difference without the mask. "I swear to you, this is the truth."

"M-m-my mom had blue eyes. I get them from her."

"Callista had green eyes. The Hale family is known for our strikingly blue eyes. It's our unique attribute, like the Grey family's crimson eyes."

"No…we aren't…it can't be…" Lily shook her head rapidly as tears gathered in her eyes. Her entire world was shattering in this moment. She struggled not to break down and sob in front of the dark witch.

"I know this is a lot to process."

Lily's tears escaped her eyes and streamed down her cheeks.

"Oh…Lily, please, don't cry." Sinestra sincerely implored. But Lily wasn't sure that she could believe it. Her misty vision didn't help her to accurately read the dark witch's facial expression.

"*Get away from her!*"

Sinestra and Lily whirled around to see Bella in the doorway, wand raised at them, a murderous look in her eyes. Sinestra's silver mask was back in place as she stepped away from Lily. The entire atmosphere in the building had changed on a dime. It was now intensely hostile.

"Isabella, don't do anything that will endanger Lily," Sinestra warned sincerely yet also at the same time sounded taunting.

"Lily," Bella ordered, "come here. If *you* so much as twitch, you're ash."

Lily got to her feet and gave Sinestra a wide berth as she rushed to stand behind Bella. Once she was there, Bella's left arm curled behind her, keeping Lily in place. For the first time since entering this building, Lily felt that everything would be OK.

"Put your wand down," Bella snarled.

"I'm afraid I can't do that, Isabella," Sinestra returned.

The two women stood unmoving in the room, just staring at one another.

"Put. Your. Wand. Down."

"No," Sinestra purred. In an instant, she shot skyward, making Lily gasp.

All the details of Sinestra vanished, as from her chest up, she was now nothing but a solid black silhouette composed of the blackest smoke Lily had ever seen. Just underneath her bust was a swirling black funnel of smoke, and black smoke was flowing off of her arms as she headed for the nearest window. Bella shot curse after curse at the black smoky mass, all of them bouncing off of shields that Sinestra put up. Just like that, the dark witch was gone. This nightmare was over.

Bella turned around and hugged Lily so tight she was having a hard time breathing, but Lily was sure she was holding on just as tightly. Today had been exceptionally trying, and Lily wanted some emotional support. But the revelation with Sinestra wouldn't leave her mind. Slowly anger was filling her up, replacing the fear that she had felt. But this wasn't the place for her and Bella to discuss this. She also needed to check on her friends and make sure they all were OK. For the moment, worry was pushing out the anger. Her friends had to be OK.

"C'mon. Let's get out of here," Bella suggested.

Lily nodded and allowed her aunt to guide her out the door, where Sierra and Sirius were standing. Sierra looked a little roughed up with several new scratches, tears in her overcloak, and bruises that were beginning to form, but otherwise fine. That was a massive relief for Lily. But she had other friends there too. There had to be more saviors than just Bella and Sirius there too, right? They were skilled, arguably the best, but they'd need extra hands just to ensure their safety and be prepared for anything they might encounter.

"The others are already back at Gerhardt, Lily. You just relax," Sirius intoned, seemingly reading her mind. He probably used *lectio animo* on her, for all she knew. He and Bella seemed gifted in that particular talent.

Lily did relax after hearing that though. Everyone was OK; they were all safe. Exhaustion overtook her as all of her adrenaline fled from her system. Sinking against Bella, she walked with them through the ruined city back to the arch. With every footstep, Lily was sinking closer and closer to sleep. By the time they did reach it, Bella was dragging Lily as unpleasant dreams of Arianna Hale swirled around in her mind.

(☆)

BLINKING HER EYES OPEN, Lily was momentarily confused as to where she now found herself. She was lying in a very uncomfortable bed in a gigantic, dimly lit room. As her eyes adjusted to the low light, more details stood out to her. Rows of beds lined the walls with white privacy curtains hovering between them via magic. The quietness of this place was also absolute—like no one was even there. This place looked vaguely familiar, but—oh. She was in Gerhardt's infirmary. She'd only been in there during the tour of the school, thankfully.

"Welcome back to the land of the living."

Lily turned at the voice, seeing Victoria lying in the bed to her left. She gave a small wave of her hand, seeing Lily looking at her.

"Vic! Are you—"

"Broken leg, mild concussion. I'm fine." She smiled at Lily and then, frustrated, blew a lock of her red hair out of her face.

"I'm—"

"No, don't apologize to me. None of us had any idea that cup was trying to kidnap you. Besides, you'll need all of your apologies in the morning. The professors are pretty angry with you."

"I know the feeling," Lily hissed as memories came back to her of Sinestra and what she had learned. "How long was I out for?"

"About six hours. My guess might be a little off, since I was out for a while too, but I think that's the closest estimate. They don't have a clock in here," Victoria grumbled.

"Are we the only ones in here?" Lily asked, looking around at all the empty beds.

"Yeah. Amara was perfectly fine, and Sierra only had some scratches and a few bruises. Scotty was a little rougher, both of his ankles being sprained, but he was released after an hour or two. They just have you here for observation, wanting to make sure that you are OK. It could've been a lot worse, all things considered."

Yes, it could have been. They could all be dead.

"Have they told you when you can leave?" Lily asked, seeing Victoria's leg in a temporary cast. She didn't know why they had even bothered with the cast since bone-healing potions were a thing and far superior to casts. Magical healing was leaps and bounds more advanced than the nonmagical means that Sierra and Scotty had told them about.

"Well…bone-healing potions take generally twenty-four hours for the strength of the bone to return to normal in my experience. So I'd say the day after tomorrow."

Lily didn't miss Victoria's statement about having experience with the bone-healing potions before or the slightly bigger glimpse she got of her friend's scar on her left inner forearm as she brushed her red hair out of her face and behind her ear. She was startled to realize the elaborateness was actually the detailed head of a snake at her wrist, its mouth open menacingly. Lily looked back at Victoria's face so as not to alert her friend to anything she had noticed, but Lily now had a lot of questions.

However, in terms of her attention, that was very low on her list. In the morning, she'd face Bella and the other professors, and Lily wanted to have salvos of her own prepared for that confrontation. She might have broken rules and stolen an amulet, but she was also betrayed by being lied to for years about who Sinestra really was.

"Well, I don't know if I'll fall back asleep or not, but good night, Vic," Lily said.

The redhead smiled at her in return. "Good night, Lily. Sweet dreams."

(☆)

SOMEHOW, LILY DID FALL asleep quickly again, and the next time she awoke, sunshine was pouring in through the windows that were present over every bed. Lily also noticed now in the daylight there was a lot of white present in the infirmary, giving it a sterile look. Victoria moaned next to her, making Lily turn her head. Victoria was getting her cast cut off by Madam Esmae. She was the only professor who wore an old-style nurse's uniform complete with an all-white nurse's hat. Lily hadn't really spoken to her a lot before, but watching her treat Victoria had Lily planning a nice conversation with the healer at the earliest opportunity. The care she had with Victoria, and with the gentleness of her touches were something that spoke great volumes to Lily.

"Now, remember, it's still weak, so you're on bedrest for another day at least," Esmae ordered, shooting Victoria a serious look.

"Yes, ma'am," Victoria replied with a nod.

"Good morning, Lily. You can leave once your aunt gets here," Esmae said with a smile at her. "She should be here momentarily."

"Thank you," Lily replied, sitting up.

"Of course, dear. I'm glad all you needed was rest. If only all the patients who come here needed that, my life would be so easy."

"Ow! Stop pulling so hard, Sierra! I can't walk that fast yet! Madam Esmae said I'd still be unsteady and weak for twenty-four hours, and it's only been eighteen!" Scotty's voice cried at that moment.

Esmae rolled her eyes and walked away, not wanting to get involved.

"Stop whining! I'm not even touching you!" Sierra bit back.

"If you're truly so concerned, we could carry you like yesterday," Amara offered.

"Oh no! Not that again! I'll get to them on my own time under my own power! No one's throwing me over their shoulder again like a sack of potatoes!"

Lily smiled at the banter as her friends rounded her curtain and then swarmed her and Victoria's beds. Once they were assured that both girls were indeed fine, they proceeded to detail the rescue mission to them, sparing nothing, and how they had to tell the teachers that they had all taken the amulet.

The cup had returned with a half-dozen Themidas and Professors Ryker, Black, Nero, Snare, and Orion, and they quickly aided Amara and Victoria. Several Venatores Mortem flew in at that moment, leading the Themidas on a chase and to a duel, the results of which were still unknown, though Lily guessed that the Venatores Mortem members escaped.

Professors Black, Ryker, and Nero raced into the city with Orion following after them. Scotty then explained how Orion and Nero freed him and carried him away—Nikki's strength stunning them. Sierra described how the black sandy figures attacked her and the two teachers as soon as they arrived. Sierra also told just how marvelous Sirius's and Bella's spellwork was in the fight. Almost like dancing instead of fighting. Then as soon as she could, Bella rushed into the temple, leaving Sirius and Sierra to finish off the last of the sandy figures.

Before Lily could go into her portion, which was the most vital in her mind, the teachers all poured into the infirmary with Bella leading the group. Sirius and Orion were behind her with Nikki hesitantly bringing up the rear. Bella sat down immediately at the edge of the bed, forcing Amara to move over to Victoria's bed, where Sierra and Scotty were already perched. Any more people on that bed, and Lily was afraid that it would collapse, or someone would fall off of it.

"Lily. We need to talk about what happened and your actions," Bella began, scowling and measuring her voice.

That was all it took. Lily's anger flared to life like a match to gasoline. It was never wise to go against the Black family temper, and Lily certainly had it.

"*My* actions? You're one to talk," Lily growled.

"What?" Bella hissed. "*My* actions? You stole the—"

"*How could you*?" Lily bellowed with sheer anger and hatred.

Bella leaned backward in shock at the outburst.

"Why didn't you tell me? Do you not really trust me?"

"Told you so," Sirius murmured behind Bella.

"Why not prepare me for who she really is? You left me completely blind! You clearly don't trust me as much as you say you do. That's the only reason that I can think of that you wouldn't tell me something like *that*!"

"Lily—" Bella tried chagrined, but Lily cut her off.

"*No*! Don't lie to me anymore!"

"I wasn't going to—"

"Had you just told me the truth, it would have kept me away from that amulet! But no, you didn't think you could trust me with such sensitive information like who Sinestra is! You didn't stop to think me finding out from her instead of *you* would shatter my world! How horrifying not knowing that damaging information was when I met her face to face!"

Bella sat on the bed in stunned silence, eyes wide as Lily went off the deep end on her. The others had discreetly moved away from them to allow the fireworks to just blow. Lily's friends looked like they wanted to be anywhere but there, and Scotty and Sierra were even looking away as Amara shielded Victoria from seeing the scene. But Lily kept her steely gaze locked on her aunt in front of her. She wasn't done with her verbal assault quite yet.

"I thought that you'd never lie to me. That I really had your complete trust. But no, I'm just a dumb, reckless child who isn't worth the effort of explaining her own past to. I'm just a nuisance that you're stuck with."

"You aren't a nuisance," Bella managed before Lily snarled.

"Clearly I am! Otherwise you would have taught me spells and wand work before I even *got* my wand! You'd have done a lot more to prepare me for my future against someone who tried to *murder* me in a rage when I was an infant! Instead, I'm virtually a lamb that was sent off for slaughter! You don't trust me, and you don't really care."

"Lily!"

"No! You don't!"

Lily threw her covers off and twisted away from Bella's attempt to grab her before she stormed away at a sprint as hot tears streamed down her face. She was mad and terribly hurt. She increased her pace as she heard Sirius stop Bella behind her. She didn't want her aunt around right now. She didn't want to be around *anyone* right now, even her friends. She needed time to calm down and process some very hard truths, truths that she should have been told by Bella and not Sinestra.

❨ ☆ ❩

"Lily? Are you OK?" Sierra asked gently when Lily finally returned late that afternoon to the infirmary. It now only held Lily's friends. Amara and Scotty were sitting on the bed that was Lily's while Sierra sat on the edge of Victoria's bed. Lily stood between the two, eyes reddened from crying and arms crossed defensively across her chest. Her bottom lip quivered as she stood there.

"No. I…I've got to tell you guys something," Lily struggled to say through a tight throat. She was barely holding herself together. For the past hour, she'd been fighting herself on whether or not to tell her friends about who Sinestra was. There were pros and cons, but in the end, she decided to tell them, no matter how painful it would be.

She trusted her friends completely, and they needed to know this. She wasn't about to mimic Bella in this act. It was the wrong thing to do. Trust meant that nothing was hidden: no lies, just the pure truth, as painful as that truth somehow was. It showed just how much a person truly was in character when they got the truth and still stood beside you.

"Go ahead, Lily," Scotty insisted.

After taking a deep breath, Lily began.

Lily explained the amulet, Sinestra being at the building, and their pitiful duel. Then she laid down the bombshell that had shattered her so completely. Everyone stared at her in shock after hearing that Sinestra was Lily's aunt. Lily felt vulnerable in a way she wasn't used to. Then Amara stood and wrapped her arms around Lily in a very comforting hug. Lily melted against her as Scotty and then Sierra joined the group hug. Even Victoria participated by grabbing and squeezing Lily's right hand. No words were spoken between them as they held that pose, just enjoying one another's company. They could have been hugging for hours, and it wouldn't have mattered. It was exactly what Lily needed.

"No matter what, Lily, you'll always have us," Amara vowed as everyone finally pulled back.

"Forever," Sierra added and smiled.

"After this year, there's no way we're splitting up. Besides, you can't choose what family you're born into. That doesn't define you. That's what my grandfather always told me." Scotty smiled.

"Wise words," Victoria mused, seemingly lost in thought. She was staring unseeingly ahead of her.

"Thank you, guys," Lily said, tearing up again. "You don't know what that means."

"Oh, don't start crying again. Then *I'll* cry," Sierra moaned.

Lily laughed and wiped her eyes as everyone smiled supportively and happily at her.

"C'mon, let's go eat dinner. I've had enough wallowing in my misery for one day. We'll be back as soon as we can, Vic," Lily promised.

"Take your time!" Victoria called after them. "I could use some peace and quiet!"

"Are you insulting our company?" Scotty asked, mock offended.

"No, just Sierra's with her nonstop trivia on literally any topic."

"Hey! It's called a useful lesson in medical potions! You could learn a lot by listening to me!"

"Relax, Sierra. We'll listen to your trivia all you want at dinner." Lily giggled.

Everyone laughed as Sierra playfully pouted leaving the infirmary. Lily noticed Sierra's pout was slowly transforming into a smile though. Her trivia wasn't that bad. It just showed that she knew a great deal… and that could be useful later on in life.

CHAPTER XVI
ANCIENT MAGIC

A week had passed since the bombshell of Sinestra's identity and Lily's epic blowout. She was still giving Bella the cold shoulder—like, Antarctica cold—only addressing her as "Professor Black" and only when she absolutely had to. It was hurting her aunt, but Lily was too angry to care and hurt herself by what had happened. She didn't like hurting Bella, but it felt satisfying to even the score a little. Despite that, she was still obsessing over her conversation with Sinestra, and the questions she had were multiplying. So, that was why Lily was walking through the hallway before dinner when she knew Bella was busy trying to wrangle those setting up game night in the common room. This was the only way Lily would be having a private conversation with Sirius.

Arriving at the protections classroom, Lily stepped inside and looked around. Sirius was in his office as usual, the walls transparent as he wrote away on a piece of parchment. Even Lily could tell that he was exhausted. The moment she reached his office door, he looked up and sighed at her. Defeat was clear in his body language.

"You want to talk," he said simply.

"Yes," Lily replied.

"Let's go for a walk then," Sirius said, rounding his desk.

Lily fell into step beside him and waited for him to signal to start. They were halfway down the hallway when the signal finally came.

"All right. What's on your mind, Lily?"

"A great many things."

"Oh joy," Sirius remarked. "Begin your opening salvo then."

"Why have wards on the amulet that can only be eliminated by a blood relative touching it?"

Based on Sirius's expression, he wasn't expecting that question to be asked right out of the gate.

"Well…" he replied slowly, "it gave us an added layer of security. Since you're her last blood relative alive, it was a smart thing to do. She's killed all the others."

"But why blood?"

There was a long pause.

"Lily, here is your first lesson in ancient magic. Blood is everything," Sirius said. "Every magical spell, curse, hex, jinx, even transportation was made possible by blood magic. It's the most powerful type of magic to employ but also the most dangerous. The harm inflicted to those involved in blood ritual magic if done improperly is catastrophic. There is, ashamedly so, some merit to blood supremacy.

"Some ancient magic is only possible for Purebloods to do because they *are* Pureblood. The magic we have and use today is severely diluted down from ancient magic. Ancient magic is way more powerful, way more temperamental, and far more complicated to wield. If you don't put in the work and effort, then it won't bend to you. Using ancient magic is a partnership. It works in harmony with you, so if it doesn't think you worthy…it won't happen."

"You make it sound like magic is alive," Lily remarked.

"It is. Through our blood, it can act and move. Magic is alive because we are alive. Many people believe that power lies in using magic that others consider dark. The truth is magic is neither light nor dark; it's just magic. How we use it dictates the light or darkness of the effect. But ancient magic is different. You're dealing with a power not many nowadays can tame."

"But you have?" Lily asked.

Sirius smirked at her in amusement. "I'm the only known master of ancient magic alive. It turns out, some of us are more open to ancient magic than others. My cousin was a master at it too before…well…I don't like to talk about it." Sirius's expression grew solemn.

"So…some people can access ancient magic easier than others," Lily summarized.

"Very much so," Sirius said, losing his unpleasant expression. "Very few though are so open. Only the most ancient of Pureblood families actually. The Ryker, Black, and Hearth families are some examples. Of course, you've probably read the list of the Sacred 200."

"I've glimpsed it," Lily confessed.

The Sacred 200 was a list of the two hundred ancient Pureblood families from North America, the UK, and most of Europe. Compared worldwide, the Sacred 200 were the only confirmed ancient families that had existed since AD 400, the beginning of the medieval times. All the ancient families elsewhere in the world were confirmed extinct around 1912 through 1945—particularly in China and Japan. So, in the eyes of the world, the Sacred 200 were the only old families left.

It gave the Sacred 200 privileges that others didn't have—like a lot of old money, lots of resources, and massive prestige for their pedigree. The families that Sirius had mentioned were members of that most esteemed group.

"I've also discovered that wand cores show it as well, even if they aren't necessarily from an ancient Pureblood family," Sirius added.

"Oh?"

"Yes. The more powerful the core, the more open to using ancient magic that person is. For example…" Sirius pulled his wand out and showed it off to Lily. It was the first time she had really examined his wand or had the chance to. It was all black with runes engraved at the grip. A gold ring similar to Lily's divided the grip from the rest of the wand, the constellation Orion engraved upon it with the star Sirius clearly visible. At the end of the grip was an engraved lily flower. "My wand."

"It looks like mine," Lily remarked, pulling out her own to compare them.

"Made by the same man, at the same time." Sirius smirked. "Mine is fifteen inches, mahogany, core of siren hair."

"Siren hair?"

"Yes. It's connected to your friend, actually." Sirius's grin widened as Lily's eyes bugged out of her head in shock and then narrowed.

"How—"

"Scylla Saint donated a couple strands of her hair long ago. They became the core of my wand. One of the unsellables of Mirando's shop."

"So, those who have Siren or Threshra hair cores are able to use ancient magic easily?"

Sirius laughed.

"Partly. Just because you have that core and are a part of that family or not doesn't mean you can use it. It only means you're more *open* to it. Using it is a whole other matter. Some must force it to happen, and others just naturally tap into it. But those more open to it have an advantage in forcing the magic to flow."

"This is so confusing," Lily groaned, making Sirius laugh again.

"You're actually following along quite well. This is advanced beyond even full-grown witches and wizards. It takes years to understand all of this. But the technical aspects of who can and cannot use ancient magic are really academic. When you're a little older, I'll teach you a little more."

"So I can use it?" Lily perked up.

"You already have."

"Not the amulet," Lily groaned.

"I'm not referring to that," Sirius said. "You used it already, and no one noticed."

"When?"

"Hallowe'en. You'd raised an ancient shield charm around you with that ogre. I was prepared to put a shield around you, but you did it first. Quite impressively, I might add. Bella just thought I did it."

She was stunned. *She* saved herself from the ogre's club and not Bella or Sirius?

They walked together silently for a few moments as Lily thought up her next question. There were so many that she was having a hard time deciding which one to ask. Arguably the one she was the most curious about since finding out Sinestra's identity was the one she ultimately decided upon.

"What do you know about my dad?"

"That's…a loaded question," Sirius said slowly. "I don't like to speak ill of the dead, but he wasn't the best man. I'll leave it at that. You'll have to find someone unbiased about him to learn more. I'm sorry, Lily."

A fair response.

"What about Arianna Hale?"

Sirius groaned in response. He'd been waiting for that one. It took him a little while before he spoke.

"She started with good intentions but quickly fell deeply into the darkest of the dark arts. She was consumed by hate and power. It goes to show that even those with righteous intent can be totally corrupted. A warning for us all."

"She never moved to kill me though," Lily argued, more confused now than before. "She just played with me. At least, looking back, that was what it felt like."

Sirius had stopped walking and was staring at her in shock. Yeah, it seemed that was happening a lot nowadays. He then looked at her determinedly.

"Lily, tell me everything that Sinestra said and her body language while saying it. Spare no detail."

And so, Lily told the story again from when she first entered the building through when she revealed her true name. Lily still didn't know why the evil witch looked so heartbroken that Lily wasn't told about her. Did she really have that big of an ego?

"Interesting…" Sirius mused. They began walking again in silence, Sirius clearly pondering the new information. Lily had more questions, but she didn't want to interrupt his thoughts, since Sirius was wearing his "don't talk to me right now" face. So, she looked around as they walked, taking in Gerhardt's halls for perhaps the hundredth time. In particular, she liked the open-air walkway that curled around the first floor of the building leading toward the bridge to the dorms. It was a new addition thanks to the attack that the Venatores Mortem had conducted. But it gave some beautiful views, so Lily didn't mind.

"Bella is sorry." Sirius spoke suddenly.

Lily looked at him with a scowl. "She lied to me."

"She was trying what she thought was the best approach to keep you safe. Even though I warned her—"

"I know. I heard your discussion at Christmas," Lily confessed.

"Then look. Bella is still learning how to be a mother too. She's already lost family once and is trying to prevent losing any more. I'm not saying it was right, it wasn't, but she's only trying to keep you safe. You're her world now. Particularly after the accident with your grandparents when you were four."

"I'm not a baby anymore. If she'd just teach me things—and *trust* me—"

"It's amazing, Lily, just how much you are like Bella." Sirius chuckled. "I think Callista would be laughing so hard at the situation she's placed her older sister in. Payback for some of their sisterly squabbles."

"Are you trying to say when she was my age she was just like me?"

"How you're acting right now is exactly how Bella acts when she's angry and venting to me," Sirius said and smiled. "Besides, you did lie to us as well. You stole the amulet with your friends and told no one. As a result, you risked the lives of yourself and your friends, along with the most powerful dark witch of our time now regaining her magic and is ready to pick up where she had left everything those twelve years ago. You were too independent in wanting to do something.

"I think that's the issue. You and Bella are so alike in so many ways that she forgets she's dealing with basically herself. If this year proves anything, it's that you very well might be exactly like us. If that's the case, then Merlin help us all."

Lily laughed at that. "You were troublesome?"

"I just might answer that one day." Sirius smiled at her, making Lily laugh harder.

She could picture Sirius and Bella running around Gerhardt as students causing trouble and chaos quite easily. At least she hadn't intentionally…well, she did go looking for that amulet. Uh, never mind.

"So you think I need to forgive her?" Lily said, returning to the topic at hand.

He nodded slowly.

"Yes. But talking things out with her is seriously needed. You need to make her aware that she has to treat you like she treats herself. Otherwise, things aren't going to improve. I personally don't want a repeat of this year."

"I…I can't do that yet," Lily confessed, shaking her head.

"You'll have to do it soon," Sirius warned. "It's better to mend things here at school versus back at Black Manor, where you're trapped. Especially given the Black family temper. The last thing that I need is to be summoned to stop the both of you from dueling."

"I'll think about it," Lily conceded. There was something else she'd been thinking about heavily the last week that she wanted to run past Bella too. But she still needed some time.

"Then that's all I can ask for. Come, I'm starved, and there's a limited supply of bread pudding tonight. If we want some, we need to be the first ones there."

Lily wasn't about to argue against that. The bread pudding at Gerhardt was absolutely to die for, and it was only offered once a month.

Together they headed for the grand mess with a quicker pace and lighter step. Lily was more than happy to call tonight a success.

CHAPTER XVII
THE PRINCIPAL

Dinner that night was one of the best that Lily had ever had at Gerhardt up to that point. She wasn't entirely sure why that was either. Maybe it was because she had spoken to Sirius and gotten some of her questions answered, or maybe it was the fact that she was indulging herself in perhaps a bit too big a portion of bread pudding, but it was lovely. Even the conversation from her fellow students who were eagerly and playfully challenging each other to games afterward was making her giddy.

Leaving the grand mess after stuffing herself with good food, Lily was looking forward to a well-earned and uneventful night playing simple games with her friends, free of stress. They were all shuffling forward in the middle of a massive group of other students of various other years as they moved through the doors of the mess chatting. Lily was half listening to Scotty and Victoria discussing their game preferences. Sierra grumbled under her breath that she'd rather read her book than play annoying games, making Lily smile. Amara, for her part, just took it in walking beside Lily contentedly. This was the perfect evening for Lily in her mind.

But it seemed Lily's night wasn't hers yet.

"Ms. Hale." She turned around, seeing Professor Orion walking toward them from the head table. As he approached, he seemed to part the flood of students behind her. "Do you mind accompanying me for a walk on the grounds?"

"Uh…sure, Professor."

"We'll save you a spot," Amara vowed and then slowly followed the other three off to the dorms. Lily could tell that she was hesitant to leave her alone, but this was Professor Orion. Lily couldn't be safer at this moment. Even at his advanced age, he was a talented wizard with a very impressive history of being a former Themida.

Now alone with the principal, Lily followed him out into the cool spring evening air.

The soothing sound of chirping crickets greeted them as they left the building, and the sounds of conversation from the students faded from the air. For several minutes, they didn't do anything but walk together, which only made Lily nervous. Was this the talk where she'd be punished for her actions? If so, why wait so long to have it? Have her think that she was free of anything, and then spring it on her just to throw her off? Was she getting detention for the rest of the year? In all of her talks with the Principal in previous years at Christmas, she had never had a conversation with him pertaining to the school, it was almost always about family and current events. Now Lily's mind was in overdrive with thoughts as to what was awaiting her for judgment. He glanced at her, making her tense up. Here it came.

"You aren't in trouble tonight," Orion intoned. "Please, relax, Lily."

"Sorry," she replied and forced herself to relax.

"Given what's happened recently, you should be. The events of this past year with you and that amulet specifically are greatly upsetting. Because of your actions, a dangerous dark witch has been released upon our world again to wreak havoc. This will be the beginning of some very trying times, and it is because of your actions, and that of your friends. Do you agree?"

Lily nodded slowly at the Principal. In a way, she supposed that her anger toward Bella was a way for her to ignore the guilt that clawed up her throat at what damage she had inflicted. She'd messed up so much with just one action with that amulet.

"However, I cannot find it in myself to punish you for your actions. Although I don't encourage first year students—or any other year for that matter—to get involved in such dangerous activities, this was not entirely your fault."

Lily whipped her head to look at the principal. There was no way that she had heard him correctly.

"Really?"

"As you know, Isabella is stubborn and prefers to handle things herself, alone. I'd hoped that she'd outgrown that fatal flaw, but it seems to have been a hope in vain. There were enough moments in her own schooling that she should have abandoned it, but as I said, she is stubborn. At least Sirius still has his uncanny control over her...or partial control. Next to Eos and Pollux Black, he's the only person that I have seen that can do that with Isabella. Even your mother and their other friends were incapable of controlling Isabella in anything."

"She should have told me," Lily said it before she could stop herself and winced.

"I agree, she should have." Orion nodded. "Instead she placed an even greater burden upon your shoulders than you were ready to receive. For that, I am sorry. You should have been prepared for that meeting and not sent into that situation blind. Never should have gone into that situation at all if we are honest. Informing you about that amulet would have made the actions you took with stealing and lying about the amulet never happen. This year, we all made mistakes, and you have paid the price in the end. I am merely thankful that it wasn't a more expensive price."

He and Lily both.

They continued walking slowly along the path to the principal's mansion as they gazed out over the field and the night that was quickly coming in over the school. On the horizon, the last rays of the setting sun could be seen in the sky. A pinkish hue was present. In another hour, the entire grounds would be bathed in moonlight and darkness. Lily's mind was focused now again on Sinestra, and there was something that she suddenly wanted to know from the principal since she had him alone—a question that just needed to be asked.

"Professor? Sinestra's more dangerous now than before…isn't she?" Lily asked.

This was a thought that had been dancing on Lily's mind ever since the amulet was destroyed. The way that she had seemed revitalized after its destruction and just how powerful she was acting when she was clearly still in a weakened state was overwhelming. She wasn't sure if even Bella could take on Sinestra if the dark witch was at her full power now. Orion slowed his walk and gazed out over the field deep in thought. He remained that way for several long moments before he finally answered her.

"I believe she is. She was always powerful, but…" He shook his head as though to clear it. Whatever it was that he was about to say, he seemed to change his mind and deem it unimportant or too much for

Lily to know at the time. Perhaps he wasn't sure about his own thoughts on the matter and wasn't comfortable theorizing without more data, particularly with a student. Lily observed him as he remained silent for a few more moments.

"Sirius has already mentioned that she will proceed with more calculation in her approaches, and I can't help but agree." He looked at Lily properly now. "Based on how your mother and your aunt have acted in the past, I suspect that you'll research into the events of the past…and your friends will undoubtedly follow you and what you do."

"Yes, I—" Lily stopped herself and bit her lip. "We know a little," Lily confessed, playing with her fingers.

Orion nodded to her as though he had known that all along and was just looking for confirmation.

"Our world had to deal with Sinestra's chaos once, and we now must do so again. Time is now scarce before the war picks up again where it left off. I'd hoped that the students of Gerhardt wouldn't have to go through that dark time again. As brief as it was before, it left its mark on all of us."

"Did you know her well when she was a student here?" Lily asked timidly.

Orion shook his head.

"No, I rarely get to know any student so closely unless they have a habit of getting into trouble. However, ones of great interest and promise I do watch. She was special in her youth, with big dreams for her future. There were others who knew her better than I ever have, including your mother, Isabella, and Sirius."

"But something happened," Lily whispered. "Her dreams were never realized."

"Several things. All of which compounded together at the perfect time, it seemed. But none of that can be changed now. History is in the past, and we must look onward to the future and deal with the events that are yet to unfold."

They walked for several more minutes as Lily's mind turned over the information she had managed to glean from the principal. This was the longest that she had ever spoken one on one with the principal before, and she got the impression he was evaluating her for something. Maybe it was just her mind making her paranoid. She had been through a lot in the recent weeks, and she was still trying to get over being kidnapped and being lied to.

"I'm curious, Lily. May I ask you something?" Orion asked.

Lily looked at and nodded to the older wizard. "Yes."

"What are your thoughts on what happened to you with Sinestra?"

"I'm…" Lily thought seriously for a moment. This was a question that she hadn't expected she would ever be asked. She needed several seconds to actually think about what had happened to have genuine thoughts on it. "I guess I'm more confused than anything. I was under the impression that she was a cold-blooded murderer, yet I'm still alive."

"Yes, that is extremely odd on her part, giving me great concern."

"Concern?" Lily asked, looking at the old man in alarm. "What do you mean?"

"I think she's become interested in you in a way she isn't with anyone else. You have gained her complete focus. I suspect that she is far from done with you. This year has been far from normal for Gerhardt, and I have the sinking feeling that there will be more abnormal years before Sinestra is defeated again."

That was what Lily was afraid of.

"But, unlike this year, these mistakes won't be made again, and you will be aware of what is occurring…provided that you and Isabella work through these issues."

"Yes, Professor."

"Lily." Orion stopped walking and faced her. "I must insist that you both work this out. Don't let there be one more horrible mistake made this year."

Lily ducked her head, feeling embarrassed. Hearing Sirius tell her to talk to Bella was one thing. But Professor Orion was something else entirely. It was like she was letting down everyone she cared about at the same time. This was the worst feeling she could imagine. She didn't dare imagine what it would be like if she disappointed him, and he gave her a disappointed look.

"I'll sleep on it, sir."

"Given your family, that's half of the battle." Orion sighed.

"I just need time," Lily tried to defend herself.

"Time is the scarcest commodity. We must use it as wisely as possible. To not do so is to hand Sinestra yet another advantage. She already has far more than she deserves, requiring us to stop her in any way possible."

Lily bowed her head. He was right after all.

"Professor?"

"Yes, Lily?"

"If my mother were in my shoes, what do you think she'd do?"

Orion looked at her, as if he were seeing some memory replay in his mind. A smirk found its way onto his face. Resting a hand on her shoulder, he gave his answer.

"She would talk to her sister. Probably use violence too, which I highly suggest you avoid. I don't need a room in this school torn to shreds. The Black sisters have fulfilled the family quota of that for several generations."

"I'll consider leaving my wand in my room then." Lily said trying some humor with the elderly wizard.

"I recommend that you do, for safety's sake." Orion nodded, his smirk now a gentle smile.

Lily smiled back at him and then bit her lip nervously. "Um, Professor? I have been wondering about something, very recently, and was curious."

"About?"

"Well, magic and blood. I know Professor Ryker told me that blood plays a part in ancient magic, but it occurs to me that I don't really know how magic came to be in the first place. I would think that it would be one of the first things that we're taught."

Orion smiled a little bigger and folded his hands behind his back.

"It's something that you learn in seventh year or the graduate program. It's in magical theory. But I shall tell you. We honestly have no idea where magic comes from. It's genetic. We know that, since it follows distinct bloodlines. But it is also random, thus the presence of Nonblood students here in our halls.

"For years, several wizards have tried to find a specific gene that makes us magical but have found nothing. I personally don't believe that there is a gene that would dictate that. I think that magic is a gift that is bestowed upon individuals. However, when it comes to bloodlines, I find myself wondering if there is a connection. If both parents of a child are wizards or witches, then the child will have magic. It's a very curious thing to research."

"So are there any people who are born into the bloodlines of magical families but don't have magic? Or have various strengths of magic?"

"No. If you are a part of a magical family, then you will have magic. As for strength of magic…there is some evidence that those that are Pureblood have stronger magic than Nonbloods. None of us understands why, and I think we never will. It will simply be one of the mysteries that can never be solved. We may not be meant to understand."

Lily nodded, somehow not surprised at the response.

"I must thank you for this evening walk, Lily. It isn't often anymore that I get to speak one on one with students just for fun. Even rarer that I get to teach a student something." His eyes twinkled in fondness, making her smile brightly at him. If her asking that question made his day, then she was happy to have obliged. "Now, if you wish to attend your game night, I suggest you return to the dorms. Your friends are surely waiting for you eagerly."

"Of course, Professor," Lily replied, a smile of her own still on her face.

Lily nodded one last time in respect to the old wizard and headed back on the trail to the dorms, thinking about their conversation. One thing was clear: she had to do something in order to get the pressure from the entire staff off of her. If the entire staff was going to pull her aside, then she definitely needed to cut it off at the pass. A mental image of Professor Presnell talking to her about the matter and then verging off onto a random lecture on some obscure thing in history made her shiver. She needed to avoid that, and there was only one thing that would do that.

She needed to have a talk with Bella.

CHAPTER XVIII
A NEW BLACK

"I've changed my mind," Lily said, trying—and failing—to break free of Amara's grasp as the siren forced her to walk to her aunt's quarters. Lily had decided after another few days to speak to her on what had happened. But now that she was actually headed there, she wanted to back out. Curse herself for telling Amara to ensure she followed through.

"You insisted tonight is the night," Amara chided.

"Yeah, well, tomorrow's a good day too!"

"Don't push off to tomorrow what could be done today," Amara retorted.

"Seriously, I don't want to," Lily protested, stopping her legs. It only stopped them for a few seconds before Amara lifted her up a few inches above the ground and kept walking. Sometimes Lily really hated siren strength.

"I made a promise, and I follow through."

"I won't fault you for breaking this one!" Lily protested, kicking her feet petulantly.

"We're here," Amara announced and set her down in front of the door.

Lily went to bolt, but Amara's hands held her firmly. After Lily stopped her squirming, Amara let her go and knocked rapidly on the door. When Lily turned to glare at her friend, the siren had already vanished, speeding down the hallway with her enhanced speed.

Now stranded, Lily gathered herself for this discussion and stared determinedly at her aunt's door. She waited in silence for a few moments before the door opened, revealing a dripping wet Bella in a fluffy black bathrobe, her black ringlets plastered to her head, a towel around her shoulders. She was scowling, but it changed to shock at seeing Lily standing there. This would be their first personal talk since the infirmary argument.

"I think it's time we talk," Lily said awkwardly.

Bella moved to the side, allowing Lily to enter, and closed the door behind her.

"So…" Bella began, sitting down on the green couch by her fireplace as she dried her hair. Whatever it was that she had begun to say, it died in the air as Lily remained standing beside the couch, looking at her.

"I'm still mad you didn't tell me who she was," Lily declared bluntly, sitting down finally on the opposite end of the couch from Bella.

She winced at that statement and lowered her head a little with what Lily would call shame. Somehow, that didn't look right for Bella to be ashamed, perhaps because that was a word that Lily would never have used with her aunt before now.

"I'm sorry. And I do care. I merely thought that information as to who she is would be a burden on you. You didn't need that."

"Not knowing was a bigger burden," Lily said it before she could stop herself.

"I'm sorry," Bella repeated, quieter this time.

Silence washed over them as Bella dried her hair with her towel. Somehow the silence was worse than their discussion.

"Aunt Bella."

Bella's eyes shot to Lily. It was the first time Lily had called her that since their argument in the infirmary, and it was a big deal in them healing the rift that had been created.

"I need to know things about me, my past, and be prepared to face things like this again. I'm just like you. Lying to me about things will only end like how this time did. I know you're probably mad at me for lying to you in turn, and probably we'll have trust issues with each other. That's only going to drive us apart. Sirius says we're the same, so do what you'd want people to do for you."

"The unbridled truth? What about your childhood innocence? I can't sacrifice that. It isn't fair to you either."

"That died when my mother died," Lily confessed.

Bella's eyes flashed with sadness for a moment at that.

"With Sinestra out there, I need to be prepared. No more keeping me in a protective bubble. That only hurt us, not helped us."

Bella removed the towel from her shoulders and twisted it nervously in her hands as she thought for a long moment, her eyes locked on the flickering flames in front of them. Lily hoped that this would go smoothly. She was really tired of fighting with Bella and wanted their normal family dynamic back. She was desperately missing it. It was at that moment that Bella sighed and looked back at her.

"You really are a mini-me." She groaned. "All right. I'll tell you everything from this moment onward, no matter how badly I want to protect you from all of the grisly details."

"Thank you." Lily sighed, feeling a weight being lifted off her shoulders. One major obstacle was overcome. Now it was time for the second—and arguably more difficult one—to commence. "I have been thinking a lot about things since we were kidnapped."

"Oh?" Bella asked, curious yet wary.

"Mostly Sinestra and what she implied about my dad."

Bella tensed and looked back at the fire now, a fire in her own eyes at Lily mentioning her dad. It wasn't a fake thing. This was Bella's true feelings. This was the first real time that Lily was seeing this.

"I never liked him much, so asking me about him isn't something you want to do, Lily."

"Sirius kind of told me as much," Lily confessed. "So I won't ask."

"Of course he told you." Bella smirked.

"But it did get me thinking. I know the Hale family is extremely wealthy but not nearly as wealthy as the Black and Ryker families. I also know it wasn't as prominent in wizarding social circles for several years before I was born. I know that their businesses are still in operation and earning a lot of money, but the people themselves don't have a lot recorded down in books, newspapers, et cetera."

"How…You and Ms. Rossi did research in the library archives," Bella deduced, her smirk growing.

"Sierra is really good at it," Lily confessed. "But that leads me to this: I'm not having any income go into my bank vault. So I'm not getting that generated income."

"Sinestra owns the businesses. You only have half of the Hale fortune, and she has the other half. It still makes you extremely wealthy though. You'd never have to work if you didn't want to. Let alone what you would inherit from me if I were to die," Bella mentioned.

"Well, that all led me to this thought." Lily stared at Bella's profile. "The Hales—that I know of—weren't good people."

"Not exactly inaccurate," Bella said with a neutral expression.

"But the Black family is full of good, kind people."

"We aren't saints, Lily." Bella glanced at her with a wry expression.

"I know. No family really is. But the last eleven generations of the Black family have done nothing but good things, helped lots of people, developed new potions, et cetera. There hasn't been anyone in the Black family who was evil or a dark arts fanatic since Castor Black. You just specialize in it and not practice it—before you try to correct me, Aunt Bella," Lily said, getting Bella to chuckle.

"OK, fair point."

"So I've made the decision to change my name to Lily Black, instead of Lily Hale."

Bella's head had never moved faster in her life. She stared at Lily in shock with her mouth agape. Lily actually was afraid that Bella had just given herself whiplash from the sudden movement. Bella's eyes had never been wider than now as she stared unmoving at Lily. OK, Lily was now afraid she might've just broken Bella. She was wondering if she should go and get Sirius to see if he could fix her as seconds turned into minutes. After five minutes of this passed, Lily finally nudged her aunt's knee.

"Um…Bella?"

"Are—are—are…" Bella closed her eyes and seemingly forced herself to focus. "Are you sure, Lily? This is a major decision on your part. It's your name."

"I'm beyond sure, Mom."

Bella's eyes snapped open again as another wave of overwhelming shock—although less than the previous time—washed over her.

"Lily…" Bella gasped emotionally.

"I don't think Callista would really mind," Lily whispered, shrinking into herself.

Truth be told, she had no idea what her mother would think of this decision. From what little Lily knew, Bella and Callista were closer than most siblings. They were also best friends. But at the same time, Sirius said they squabbled. But what set of siblings didn't squabble from time to time? Would she really be OK with Lily calling Bella her mom instead of her? Sure, they looked eerily alike and could pass as mother and daughter easily, but Callista gave birth to her. Would this be crossing a line? Should she take it back? The more she dwelled on this, the more she questioned herself.

But that uncertainty vanished when Bella scooted herself right beside Lily and hugged her completely and tightly. With Lily's face at Bella's neck, she was enveloped in warmth, Bella's unique scent, and lavender from her favorite shampoo.

"She wouldn't have minded at all, Lily. Not given the circumstances," Bella said with a watery voice.

"I love you, Mom."

"I love you too, Lily." There was a pause before Bella let out a frustrated sigh. "Damn you, Callista."

"Wha—"

"She bet that she'd get me to melt with you despite my best efforts. I hate it when she wins bets!" Bella snarled but without the bite. "Well, at least I don't have to buy her a new invisibility cloak. That child one I accidentally tore worked just fine."

"She had an invisibility cloak?" Lily asked, stunned.

Bella nodded. "Yeah, one meant for kids to use, not a real invisibility cloak. Not truly invisible, but it did obscure you pretty well. Then it was burned by her worthless husband because he was suspicious."

Bella stopped herself from saying more, but Lily saw clearly that her father and Bella had been enemies in the past—or at the very least resented the other's mere existence. Lily sidled up to Bella again, casting thoughts of anything but this perfect moment away. She was content for the first time since Christmas and wasn't letting this moment go for anything—not even for a bribe involving sweets and chocolate. Lily might even hex the person if they tried.

"Can I spend the night here? I know it's against the rules, but—"

"I can look past it for one night since Professor Black isn't here right now," Bella joked playfully, making Lily smile and melt into her more.

Right then, Lily was glad that Amara had forced her to come there. This was perfect, and Lily wouldn't have changed a thing.

(☆)

"Lily Black. I like the sound of it," Scotty said through the mirror as Lily and her other friends huddled around it on Victoria's bed. It was only the second time they'd used it, but it was already a very useful tool at their disposal. Scotty could now be involved in their late-night conversations if he wanted to, and he did want to. He just completed their group, but they could also now enjoy the comforts of their dorm room as they chatted.

"Somehow it rolls off the tongue easier," Sierra playfully joked with a broad smile.

"It's more fitting," Amara said, twirling one of her red curls around her finger.

"Thanks, but it's just a name," Lily said, shrugging.

"It's not just a name. Lily, you act like what a Black should be like!" Scotty argued. "You *are* a Black and never were a Hale if your other aunt is anything to go by."

"Speaking of, that'll be my new personal project. I have to know everything about Sinestra, the Hales, and the war that is possible for me to know. I could use you guys' help," Lily said, folding her legs again.

"I can ask my mom what she knows," Scotty volunteered. "Like the Hale family and how they were."

"I could ask Grandma about the war, although I might not get much," Amara added.

"Anything is better than nothing," Lily assured her.

"I'll try and research but no promises," Sierra said.

"That's all I'm really asking right now," Lily reassured them.

"Can we keep in contact over the summer?" Victoria asked. "I'll miss this too much if we don't."

"Like you'd realistically be able to ignore my letters," Lily scoffed. "Nothing is going to break us apart."

"I'll second that," Scotty said and smiled in the mirror.

"My letters might be few and far between. The magical post doesn't go underwater," Amara warned.

"Mine might be sparse too. My parents have us traveling this summer," Victoria said, sounding and looking depressed.

"That doesn't sound too bad." Sierra said.

"To visit family. Or those they consider family." The way Victoria was saying it implied they weren't family at all, and she really didn't like them.

No one commented. They all allowed the conversation to shift.

"I doubt it'll happen anytime soon, but you guys should come to Black Manor for a sleepover of sorts. We could even all head to Gerhardt together as a group," Lily suggested.

"I'd be *so* down for that!" Sierra beamed.

"Translation, Sierra would just come to stay locked away in the manor's gigantic library," Lily teased.

"Gigantic…*library*?" Sierra's eyes twinkled.

"Oh boy, here we go." Victoria giggled.

"There's even a lovely fountain in the entryway." Lily smirked, looking at the siren.

Amara straightened her back at the mention of a fountain.

"Fountain?"

"And a full-scale Verona pitch. Turns out Aunt Bella was a star player while here."

"Full scale?" Scotty salivated.

"Um…" Victoria looked at them all in their dream states. "Guys?"

"Dream about my home later. Talk now."

"Can we make reservations right now?" Sierra asked sweetly, causing everyone to burst out laughing.

Lily was positive that when this sleepover did happen, she'd be corralling them the entire first day. But it would be worth it. Her friends were worth anything.

CHAPTER XIX
GERHARDT CUP

It felt like the school year had flown by them. To Lily, it seemed like only yesterday that she'd arrived at Gerhardt with Bella for the first time and was settling into her dorm room as Bella had hung out in the doorway watching her with excitement in her eyes. Now it was their last night at the school for the year. The following day, they'd all leave for home to enjoy their summer off with family. Graduation for the seventh years and the graduate program students would be tomorrow evening after everyone else had left, so they could have their moment of glory without a few thousand younger students gawking at them. Lily was thankful Bella didn't have to stay for that ceremony this year, because Lily really didn't feel like sitting around for that.

Most of their belongings had already been packed away so only the bare essentials were out and available for them to use. Via a pure luck lottery draw, Lily was the one selected to hold on to the other half of Scotty's mirror. Well, sort of. Since Amara was underwater—and nude all the time as a result—and Victoria was traveling, the only ones able to hold on to it over the summer were Lily or Sierra. A rock-paper-scissors showdown later and Lily had it with her belongings.

"Hey, whose is this?" Victoria asked, holding up a T-shirt with an owl on the front of it.

"Oh mine. I thought I'd already packed that away," Sierra said, taking it from Victoria's hand.

"How did we obtain three different bath mats?" Amara demanded from behind Victoria in their bathroom. Lily got off her bed to see what it was that the two redheads were doing in there.

"What are you two—" Lily's voice stopped at the sight of Amara twirling her fingers with spouts of water following her commands to clean the shower area down.

Sure enough, at her feet were three bath mats in the small bathroom. Victoria was using her wand and drying them individually. Despite the cramped quarters and the show that Amara was putting on, the bathroom's cleanliness was *incredible*.

"Oh! That's right! You never saw this after Hallowe'en!" Sierra said behind Lily in the bathroom doorway. Lily looked at the bookworm.

"*This* is how our room was cleaned?" Lily couldn't stop herself from gawking at the scene again.

"The school servant elves tried to clean it, but when they all began puking and fainting from the smell one by one, Amara took charge." Victoria shrugged.

"OK. I clearly still have a lot to learn about you, Amara," Lily admitted.

The redheaded siren smiled her perfect toothy smile at Lily before returning her attention to the shower once more. Lily stepped back and around Sierra, who was also moving back to her own bed now, and allowed the two redheads to clean away to their hearts' content.

However, she hadn't forgotten the question that had brought her to the bathroom in the first place.

"As for the bath mat issue, I haven't a clue as to how we obtained three of them."

"Perhaps someone sneakily placed a duplication charm on them," Amara suggested.

"They're all different, look," Victoria spat.

Lily shook her head, smirking, and headed back to her bed and half full suitcase.

"Is it bad that I already miss you guys and we haven't even left yet?" Sierra asked, sounding a little down as she tossed her owl T-shirt into her suitcase.

"No, I'd call that a good thing. It means that we really care for one another," Lily responded, throwing the last set of her school robes into her own suitcase. With that, she zipped up her suitcase, her job completed. She was packed except for the items that she would use in the morning and her school overcloak.

"Who brought ocean-spray-scented body lotion, and why is this the first time I'm seeing it? I would've used this!" Victoria whined.

Lily pouted too because she'd have loved to use it as well.

"Mine. Now I know what to get you next Christmas." Amara giggled.

"Vic and me!" Lily pleaded.

Amara's laugh echoed from the bathroom. "All right, both of you. Sierra?"

"I'll pass, but thanks."

(☆)

"A LITTLE MORE TO the left…a little more…Stop! That's too far now. Bring it back this way a bit. Whoa! Too much! I said a bit, not the length of a broom!"

Lily and her friends sat at the first-year table watching the newest graduating banner get set into place. Professors Bloodstone and Ryker were levitating it as Professor Samsona—head of that year—directed them. "Back some more."

"We have it centered to the room's view. Can we just secure it?" Bloodstone asked.

"It must be perfect. Anything else is unsatisfactory," Samsona argued.

"No wonder we were drafted. We're the only ones willing to deal with this."

"Quit your complaining, Sirius!" Samsona chided. "There! Secure it!"

"Gladly," both men muttered in unison.

Bella leaned in next to Lily and gazed up. Based on the smirk she was wearing, Lily knew she was going to have some fun—at Sirius's expense.

"It's crooked, just so you know."

"What?" Professor Samsona gasped in horror and spun to look. Sirius and Drifus shot Bella death glares.

"It's perfectly fine, Poppy. No need to continue to torture your peers." Professor Orion chuckled.

Sirius walked past them, allowing Lily to hear his "jerk" remark to Bella.

The grand mess was filled with chatter from everyone gathered bidding friends goodbye or seeing what career paths those graduating were going off on. Unlike normal or on the weekends when they would be in their leisure clothes, everyone was wearing their Gerhardt overcloaks over their normal clothes, the colors of their individual years lining the inside. Breakfast had officially ended an hour before, but everyone remained to hear who would win the Gerhardt Cup that year. After that, they'd be leaving with their families for the summer. Lily had no idea where their year fell in the standings, but she'd guess pretty low.

Finally, Professor Orion quieted down the hall.

"Students and soon-to-be graduates, this year has been extraordinary," Orion began. "Despite all the trials, tribulations, and near-death experiences…"

Lily and her friends shifted in their seats.

"…this year has been one of the best and happiest in my long memory. On behalf of all the staff, I thank you all for the treat of this year."

Applause filled the mess from students and teachers alike.

"In a historical moment, this year's year points for the Gerhardt Cup was extremely close, showing all of your hard work. For the first time in over a century, the first place position is claimed *not* by the seventh years…having been beaten out by a mere two points."

The seventh years deflated at their table, a few graduate program kids giving them "there, there" pats on the shoulder.

"Since the graduate program doesn't earn points and its students are ineligible to compete for the cup, in seventh place with 1,051 points is the fourth-year class…who would've been higher had they not misbehaved so much this past week."

They shrank down in their seats under the principal's disappointed gaze.

"In sixth place, with 1,125 points, is the second-year class. A vast improvement from your 472 points last year."

"At least we beat them," Scotty murmured.

Lily agreed. They had already surpassed two grades, and she was expecting that they would be in last place. This was far better than she had imagined.

"In fifth place, with 5,700 points, is the fifth-year class. Tied for third and fourth are the third years and then the sixth years at 11,341 points."

Lily straightened in her seat as realization sank in. Everyone else in the mess was having the same epiphany too as all of the eyes in the room now drifted to the first-year table. Two spots remained for two years…and seventh didn't sit in first place. It didn't take a genius to put the tremendous conclusion together.

"In second place with 11,500 points is the seventh-year class. And finally, in first place with 11,502 points is the first-year class. The class of 2017 has the highest points earned in their first year on record. Congratulations on earning the cup!" Orion finished just as a standing ovation kicked into full gear.

Lily was positive that she was in shock. Her fellow first years were in shock. They'd just won the Gerhardt Cup. She watched almost in a trance as Bella took the elaborate cup from Professor Sybil Sterling, the divination teacher—who honestly looked like a hippie lady complete with an old tie-dye shirt—and showed it off to all of the first years. Lily was snapped out of her strange stupor by Scotty's snort.

"Next year's going to be a lot tougher. Everyone will be gunning for this cup."

"Relax, Halifax! We'll beat 'em again!" a boy down the table from them said excitedly.

"With attitudes like that, along with hard work, you will," Bella said, coming down the table.

Most of their year spoke up excitedly at that. Sierra, however, huffed. "I should get an award. Or a ribbon at least. Most of those points came from me."

"Your award is our friendship, Sierra," Victoria said, nudging the bookworm's shoulder.

"Well…I guess that isn't really a bad award to have."

"Of course it isn't," Lily piped up sincerely. "Besides, you're number one in our eyes, Sierra."

Another forty minutes passed by in easy conversation before all of the professors finally ushered everyone outside to where the horde of waiting parents were gathering. Lily stayed with her friends in a mob, winding their way through the masses of people until they ran into— almost literally—Sierra's parents first.

Mr. and Mrs. Rossi were extremely nice people, if slightly over-whelmed with wonder at what their lives now contained. Lily found out through talking with them that they were a Doctor and a Dentist respectively. They were thin, brown-haired, and wearing warm, loving smiles. Sierra was hands down a younger version of her mom but with her dad's eyes and smile. They headed off with Sierra promising to write soon.

Then the remaining group members turned their attention to find-ing the next parent. She happened to be standing a few feet away, talking happily with Sirius, who was smiling himself.

The woman was drop-dead gorgeous, like an older version of Ama-ra, but instead of green eyes, this woman's were piercing amethyst, and her red curls fell to her hips instead of the midback like Amara's. Then there was the curve-hugging red dress she was wearing.

"That's Grandma. I'll write to you all soon," Amara vowed, rushing off with a smile.

"Scotty!" a woman's voice called, gaining their attention.

"Mom! Bye, guys. You'll see my letter soon!" He rushed off and hugged his mom. She was fairly tall, blond hair curled to her shoulders with brown eyes. It was clear that she was wearing some makeup, but nothing that was over the top. She looked over at them as he reached her, her Magical Congress robes still on her, and they disapparated away. By the time Lily looked back, Amara and Scylla were gone. Even Sirius had faded away into the crowd. Another time, then.

Lily and Victoria meandered together for a few more minutes before Victoria stopped and whimpered slightly. Lily was confused and was just about to ask her what was wrong when she followed the redhead's gaze through the crowd.

Although the couple wasn't dressed in the most expensive and lavish black robes, they were definitely of a very fine quality. They looked immaculately put together from afar and would seem pleasant enough if not for the scowls they wore and the glares they were shooting at everyone. In fact, they looked really angry to even be there.

The woman was an older and a bit meaner-looking version of Victoria, an air of haughtiness flowing off of her as she seemed to sneer at everyone around her. It was like she was used to being around people that she considered decent and not those who were at present around her…and ignoring her. Her similarly straight red hair was pulled back into a bun, allowing Lily to see the intricate gold earrings that she was wearing.

The man beside her had long flowing black hair that easily fell to below his scapulae, and he was clean-shaven. He appeared a little paler than normal, but given some jobs of working indoors for long hours, that wasn't too uncommon, particularly in the Magical Congress. He had a walking stick in his hands that had silver and chrome highlights on the black wood. Lily could tell, even from this distance, that the handle of the stick was of a silver skull. A bit macabre.

"Um, I should head over to them alone. Bye, Lily," Victoria timidly said.

Lily grabbed her arm lightly, halting her. "Bye Vic. Remember, write when you can."

"I will," she replied with a smile and then slinked over to her parents after Lily let her go.

A short, terse conversation later and the three disapparated away.

Now alone, and beginning to feel a little claustrophobic, Lily headed back to the mess in search of Bella. It should be easy to find her since there weren't that many dark-haired, corseted witches present at the school currently. Well, there were other Pureblood women wearing corsets, but Bella should stand out…maybe? Looking around her, Lily realized that there were more than a few who could vaguely resemble Bella from behind. Oh, Merlin, this wasn't going to be as easy as she was thinking it would be.

(☆)

"ARE YOU READY TO go?" Bella asked as Lily grabbed her suitcase from the elves who were watching over it for her.

Lily nodded and gripped Bella's arm for them to apparate back home. The familiar sensation washed over her, and they appeared in the entryway of Black Manor once more. Lily breathed a sigh of relief as her body automatically relaxed at being home again.

"Lily?"

"Yes?" she asked, her foot hovering over the bottom step of the grand staircase.

"There's something we need to talk about that we haven't yet," Bella said, resting her hands lovingly on Lily's shoulders.

"What is it?" Lily asked, furrowing her eyebrows. She thought that they'd talked through all they needed to in Bella's quarters. So what didn't they cover?

"You were right, Lily; I should've prepared you for facing Sinestra no matter how remote that possibility seemed to me. I should have taught you a lot of things about dueling before you began your schooling at Gerhardt."

Lily turned around to see her aunt's guilt-ridden face. "Really?"

Bella nodded. "Truth is, I was afraid of teaching you too much and making it look like favoritism. So I just didn't bother. That could very well have gotten you killed this year. It…it's a mistake I'm not repeating ever again."

"Are you…" Lily really didn't want to get her hopes up too high just yet. This could still go in a different direction, and the best thing she could do was just sit tight and wait it out to hear what it was that Bella was thinking. Bella smirked at her, clearly reading her mind as to her hesitation.

"I'm saying, Lily, as of tomorrow morning, your private lessons on magic and protections begin. You're not going to be so underclassed the next time Sinestra sees you. In fact, she'll get quite the nasty surprise."

Lily beamed at that and could honestly say that this summer was going to be so much more fun than she had initially imagined it would be. She would be spending the entirety of it with Bella, learning dueling from her, and would be able to give her evil aunt a big surprise if she ever tried to kidnap her again. This would be awesome!

"I can't wait," Lily replied with a brilliant smile. "What time will we start?"

ABOUT THE AUTHOR

When he's not writing, Ethan Holiday is often found doing small projects for his parents' home, where he currently resides in Dexter, Michigan, while attending college.